The Last Family of Wizards

Other Books by Ron Cook

The Mountain Dulcimer

Onward Through the Fog: Short Stories & Mystery Novelettes

A Young Upstart: Poetry & Contour Drawings 1977-1982

On Guard in the General's Chorus: Army & Korea Stories 1966-1968

Firebrand: A Charles Blue Mystery #1

The Last Family of Wizards: A Charles Blue Mystery #2

The Last Family of Wizards

A Charles Blue Mystery

Ron Cook

The Last Family of Wizards

Copyright © 2023 Ron Cook

First Edition

All rights reserved. This book or any portion thereof may not be reproduced or used in any manner whatsoever without the express written permission of the publisher except for the use of brief quotations in a book review.

This is a work of fiction. Any references to historical events, real people, or real locales are used fictitiously. Other names, characters, places, and incidents are the product of the author's imagination. Any resemblance to actual events, locales, or persons, living or dead, is entirely coincidental.

Paperback ISBN: 979-8-9857889-2-1
eBook ISBN: 979-8-9857889-3-8

www.roncook-author.com

Printed in the United States of America

I dedicate this book to my wife, Stella. Again, thank you for your support and cheerleading for my books.

And another thanks to Julie Tibbott. Your editing helped me immensely.

Prologue

The 1989 earthquake devastated Santa Cruz. It was two months since the big Loma Prieta shaker, and the ground still moved with smaller and smaller aftershocks. Some of the more recent dwellers, mainly out-of-state University of California Santa Cruz students, would freak out with each little temblor. Longtime residents took the light bumps in stride. After all, we were only a few miles from the infamous San Andreas Fault, and those of us who grew up in the area were used to an occasional movement of the ground. However, the big one we had two months ago was too much for everyone.

Several blocks of Pacific Avenue, affectionately known as the Pacific Garden Mall, were still closed off for the demolition of buildings that collapsed or were red tagged as unsafe. A block away six large tent-like structures had been erected in three parking lots where the displaced shops were able to set up and sell communally inside them.

One building that survived the downtown mayhem was the Catalyst, a bar, restaurant, and entertainment venue on lower Pacific Avenue. This building had very little damage, and, after the place was deemed safe by building inspectors, it reopened. The owner wanted to cheer things up, so he decorated the establishment for the upcoming Christmas season with colored lights both inside and outside.

It was a Saturday night, and the Catalyst was putting on a fundraiser to help out those who had homes and stores damaged or lost in the earthquake. Three local bands had volunteered to play: The Rubbers, a punk band; Cease and Desist, an electronica duo; and the headlining band, The White Friars, who had recently released their second progressive rock album on Electra Records. The event sold out.

Each band did well that night, performing their best for the standing room only crowd. By the time The White Friars finished their second encore, even with the crowd asking for more, it was nearly 1am and management had to shut down the music and get ready to close. It was time to pack up and go home.

The White Friars was a father and son band. The father, known as the bassmeister, was Del Prentiss, who claimed he was thirty-nine, for the young ladies in the audience, but was really forty-six. His son, known as The Shredder, real name Marty Prentiss, lead guitar, was twenty, as were the keyboardist and drummer. They played songs that Del had written years ago and many his son had recently penned for the second album.

Even though their two albums sold well, they never opted to

pay for roadies. No need to. Between Del and his son and their very simple incantation, the only one they knew, their equipment could be as light as feathers. For them. Not for the other two band members who grunted lifting and moving the heavy amplifiers and drums.

Del had been playing in bands, some good, some bad, for over twenty-five years. His recent band with his son was the first that did well. He was happy.

The first band he was in, Black Mischief, was terrible. He knew it was bad from the start and tried to improve it, writing several of the songs. Unfortunately, bad warlock Pete Ramahi insisted on emulating the Doors, but their lead singer, a skinny Jim Morrison clone, couldn't sing. He just pranced around yelling Del's lyrics into the microphone. Usually, Pete played his rhythm guitar so loud, the rest of the band had to turn up to be heard. The clone's singing couldn't be heard at all. Pete kept reciting incantations to make the audience think they were listening to a great rock band. Del tried to discourage Pete's spells, but Pete was too powerful and always seemed so angry. A few times Del tried to ask him why, but Pete never talked about it.

Del has often wondered where his other old band members ended up. Especially when things got out of hand with Pete, who tried, through even more incantations, to get Black Mischief a recording contract with Columbia. His spellbound record company contact wanted a demo to take to his boss and paid for their time at Hyde Street Studios in San Francisco. What Pete couldn't do was use his abilities to make the recordings sound good. Black Mischief took an eight-hour block of time to record only one song. And it sounded terrible, no matter what spells Pete tried to do. Columbia wanted nothing to do with the band after that. Del, frustrated and angry, quit. The band broke up, and Del lost all contact with the other members. He headed back to San José, then soon moved to Santa Cruz to be with his girlfriend, who became mother to Marty and to his sister, Dria a few years later.

By the time all the White Friars' equipment was broken down and moved from the stage to their vans, it was nearly two o'clock. Del and Marty closed up the side doors of their old classic customized 1957 VW van behind the Catalyst. The other two band members had already left in their own 1950 Ford woody station wagon. From what the band made on record sales and concerts the last year, they were able to purchase their dream cars.

Marty got in the van behind the steering wheel and waited for his dad who went back into the "Cat" to get the birthday gift he purchased that day for his eighteen-year-old daughter, Dria. He had forgotten it in the dressing room. The security guard followed him and told him to hurry. He wanted to lock up. He escorted Del to the back exit.

Marty had started the van to warm up the engine. He glanced in his rearview mirror and saw a light coming up behind him. He thought it was another car coming into the parking lot with its high beams on, nearly blinding him. But it got bigger and closer until it engulfed the VW bus.

There was a flash.

Then there was an explosion.

The blast blew out the windows in a couple of cars in the lot and several buildings in the neighborhood. It blew in the back door to the Catalyst, knocking the security guard back into Del. The guard was knocked out. Del, in shock and injured, jumped up and ran out to the parking lot. There he saw his son's VW bus burning in a bright white flame. The flame died out almost instantly, leaving the bus and all its contents in a pile of twisted metal and smoking ash.

Chapter 1

Even with all the earthquake repairs going on throughout San Francisco, I was fortunate I was able to hire a good architect and contractor to work on the restoration and remodel of my Victorian home on Page Street in the Haight-Ashbury district.

Because work on the big house would take eight to ten months, according to the contractor, Bell and I moved down to my small Pleasure Point home in Santa Cruz. I was unsure if Bell would want to come back to this place, because the last time she was here was when Granny had dropped her off after her twenty-year death sleep. When she arrived, she looked the same age as when she was put to sleep in the Telegraph Hill caves by that evil warlock Pete Ramahi. Every time Bell went to sleep and woke, she would advance years until she finally reached the age she should be. The same as me.

Crud. Am I that old now? Forty-five?

I didn't need to worry. Bell told me it was no problem for her. She was very happy we finally got back together. I was too. I always felt we were soulmates. Even through a shaky relationship start when I was in college, we definitely loved each other.

On our first Saturday back in Santa Cruz, we drove to Cabrillo College for the Aptos Farmers Market to get some good organic vegetables. Bell hadn't been to a farmers' market before and enjoyed seeing everything that was available, even in mid-December. She bought more vegetables than we would be able to eat in a week. Not much fruit was available this time of year except for oranges and lemons. One vendor still had persimmons, both Fuyu and Hachiya. Bell had never eaten persimmons, so I bought a couple of both varieties. The Fuyu could be sliced and eaten hard, while the Hachiya had to ripen more until very soft to eat. Another vendor had dried Blenheim apricots, another fruit that Bell had never tasted. I bought one bag for us to nibble on.

"Charles!" Bell exclaimed as we were heading back to our van with all our purchases. "These apricots are great! Give me some more!"

"Uh... Bell, don't eat too many at once. You could get a stomachache... and probably need to go to the bathroom... a lot."

"Really? But they taste so good."

"Believe me. I'm the voice of experience. My parents would bring dried fruit home all the time. When I was ten or eleven, I ate so many prunes and dried apricots I was stuck in the bathroom for hours."

"Ugh!" Bell made an 'oh yuck' face and we both laughed.

After we got home and put all our purchases away, we sat down at the dining room table with some coffee, and I picked up that day's Santa Cruz Sentinel newspaper, which I hadn't read yet. The headline mentioned the ongoing investigation into a car explosion and suspicious disappearance of a young musician in the parking lot of the Catalyst the week before. I wasn't thinking much about it until I got almost to the end of the article where it mentioned his father and sister. It also gave a little history of the band and the albums they released.

"Bell. Take a look at this. See this guy's name? Oh. Sorry. That's right. You didn't know anyone I was associated with during my band days. Anyway, love, I remember this guy. He was in a band with our old enemy Pete Ramahi in the 1960s. Yeah. I know. Pete was trying to get at me then too. Anyway, this guy had powers of some kind but never used them like Pete did back then. In fact, I saw him more than once try to convince Pete to stop casting spells. Delwood. Yes, Del. The paper said it was his son who was in that explosion. I wonder…"

"You think it might have been some kind of black magic?"

"Hard to say, but people with abilities like ours can get targeted, as we found out with Pete. Evidently, this young guy, Marty it says here, his mother predeceased him. I wonder if she had any abilities. Hmm. I wonder what she died of."

"Charles, I sense that you want to investigate. Cool it, honey. Why don't we relax and enjoy our quiet time here in your little beach house for a while."

The following day, Sunday, our quiet time barely got started. One o'clock, while we were finishing our lunch of grilled tuna and cheese sandwiches, we heard a scratching at the front door. I opened it to find a large pure white cat, a tail-less long-haired Manx, sitting there staring up at me.

"Bell. Come here. Take a look at this beautiful cat."

It spoke to me in a female voice telepathically. "*Thank you for your kind words. Mister Blue, I presume. I am Freesia. Madam sent me to invite you and Miss Beltane to tea on her boat at the yacht harbor, dock E, slip 5, at four o'clock. May I tell her you will come?*"

Bell and I were taken aback by the sudden appearance of a talking cat. It asked again, "*I repeat. May I tell her you will come?*"

I snapped out of it, speaking back telepathically. "*Uh… First, who is madam?*"

"*I was not asked to tell you that. I… ah. She contacts me now. Yes, Madam, I understand. Her name is Madam Seren. Now. May I tell her you will come?*"

I looked at Bell and she nodded yes. Both of us were curious.

"*Yes,*" I answered. "*We will come.*"

Exactly at four, we walked down the boat ramp to the dock E gate. It was locked, and Bell was about to use her unlocking incantation, when the wire gate opened by itself. We entered and walked down the sloping ramp to the dock and up to slip 5, near the end.

Moored there was a large craft that looked like a converted fishing boat. Sitting on the wheelhouse roof was the white cat, Freesia. "*Come aboard. Madam is below.*" The cat pointed to an open door with its paw. We stepped aboard and walked down a short steep stairway into a galley. Sitting on a bench seat at a small built-in table at the end of the galley was Madam Seren. She smiled and waved us over to sit across from her. She looked Granny's age, but thinner, and maybe taller. But that was hard to tell with her sitting down. Her long gray hair was pinned up into a rounded bun. No gypsy-style clothing for her, like Granny sometimes wears. She was dressed in jeans, a white fishermen's knit sweater and dark brown ankle high hiking boots. Obviously dressed for the chilly ocean breezes typical in the yacht harbor in the Winter. She also wore round glasses in a thick tortoise-shell frame.

"Ah, Mister Blue and Miss Beltane. So happy you accepted my invitation." She reached over and shook our hands. Bell spoke first.

"Thank you so much. I'm pleased to meet you. But please call me Bell."

"Yes. Thank you. Me too. And please call me Charles."

Madam Seren leaned back and laughed. "I am sorry. I am so used to being formal. I mean with my clients, of course. And please, call me Gwyn. Sit back and relax. The tea is ready. Let me pour."

With Bell's experience with a tea that Pete Ramahi used to put her into a death sleep, she looked at the tea with trepidation. Gwyn noticed. "Do not worry Miss… Bell. I do not brew my own teas. This is my favorite. Lipton Orange Pekoe. I get it at Shopper's Corner."

"Madam Seren… Gwyn, how did you know I was nervous about the tea?"

"I can see in your mind your concern, and I see what had happened to you."

I took a sip of tea. *Yes, Lipton. It's good, Bell.*

Bell spoke. "Thank you for the tea. Gwyn. I can tell you are a seer. A real clairvoyant. Aren't you?"

"Well, yes. I knew you would be able to tell. What else can you see in me Miss… sorry. Bell?"

Bell looked straight into her eyes. "Well, I see you are a good person," Bell said. "You've lived on this boat for two years now. You like helping people, especially people who have abilities that are in trouble. You lived in San Francisco. Really? You must know…"

Gwyn cut in. "Of all the gods and goddesses, you are quite the all-seeing witch. You must have a psychic in your background. Charles, I have heard so much about you and Bell. I just had to meet you both. Oh… by the way, good work on that evil Ramahi fellow."

I asked, "You know about that?"

"That much power and evil does not stay in one place. There are those of my kind, well, those of us who are left, who envisioned and felt that terrible Ramahi disturbance for many, many years. Father, mother, son… oh, and some followers too. So many fires." Gwyn looked down and sighed, then continued. "Unfortunately, feeling it is one thing. Trying to help combat evil is another. It is something we cannot do. My kind are seers. Psychics. Life readers. We are not able to spellbind. We all breathed a sigh of relief when you dispatched that psychotic warlock."

"But what about your familiar, Freesia?" Bell asked. "Isn't that a spell you made that allows her to talk?"

"First, Freesia is not my familiar. Our kind do not have familiars. And Freesia is not the result of a spell I cast. Like I said,

I cannot cast spells. She was spellbound by one of the Ramahi family nearly twenty years ago and left for dead. When she found me at my old place of business in San José, she was near death. I took her in to feed and protect her. She has stayed out of loyalty. We both hoped someone, like maybe you, Charles, would come and possibly return her to her human form."

"Who was she before?" Bell asked. "Was she one of us?"

"Yes, she was. And still is in her current form. It was her who unlocked the gate for you. Freesia Diehl was a young witch and barely seventeen when the Ramahi clan killed her parents by fire, a lot like what happened to your parents, Charles, I am sorry to say. She confronted them about the murders and tried to put a curse on them, but her high young voice reminded the Ramahi mother of a screeching cat, so she cast a spell turning her into what you now see. So, tell me, Charles. Are you able to reverse a very old spell?"

"I might be able to. Maybe my shaman side can heal her and bring the real Freesia back. I may have to consult with my grandfather's spirit. Or maybe I'll ask my grandmother first."

"Ah, yes. Peter Red Feather and Yana. I was so sorry to hear of Peter's passing. And Yana. Bell, you were going to ask me if I knew Yana Blue. Yes. I know her well. A very powerful woman and someone who can naturally block psychics like me." Gwyn smiled at the memory. "Yana and I met in San Francisco at her fortune telling business by the old Playland at the Beach. So funny. My fortune telling was… well, legitimate. Yana's was made up for the Playland tourists. However, when I found out what Yana really was, we became very good friends. We occasionally met at her Mystic Eye store for tea. Is she here in

Santa Cruz too?"

"No," Bell answered. "She is still in the City arranging to sell the Mystic Eye building. Well, actually, the property. The shop was damaged in the earthquake last October and will probably be demolished. There'll probably be a lot of rebuilding in the area now that the Embarcadero freeway is going to be torn down. She's planning to buy a house from an old friend who is planning to move to England next year."

"Ah. I wish her well. I really should visit her one of these days. Now. I have one more thing I need to discuss with you. But first, let us finish our tea. Biscuit?"

Chapter 2

"Have you heard about that car explosion at the Catalyst Friday night? You have. You read about it in yesterday's paper. I also see you knew Del Prentiss from... Ah. Yes. It was the band he was in with that bad piece of work, Pete Ramahi. Let me see." Gwyn closed her eyes. "Ah, yes, not a good band. Mister Ramahi forced his way into the band and took over leadership. Mister Prentiss was the only decent musician and was the only one from that group who continued to play in bands through the years."

Gwyn's visions were bringing up things that I never knew about, and really didn't want to know about. At that time, I had no idea Pete was out to get me. I thought he was just being a warlock jerk. That thought made me question. "Gwyn. Is Del a Ramahi follower?"

"Heavens no, Charles. Del is a lovely, caring person... and a good father. Also, he has hardly any powers. He cannot even cast a protection spell. He is very upset his son disappeared and might have died."

"Might have died?" I questioned.

"I am unsure. My senses about the death of young Marty do not... how do you say...compute. Anyway, to continue, I have known Del for several years. He came to me shortly after his wife disappeared. Another strange happening, but one I could not sense at all for some reason. I am still trying to find out what happened to her. Maybe..." Gwyn paused, looked down at her tea, then looked back up and continued. "Well. Now I want to find out what happened to his son."

"Can you sense what happened this time?" asked Bell.

"All I can see in my mind is a white light. White light and black magic."

"Could this have been an attack by some Ramahi follower?" I asked.

"No. I am sure of that. When you destroyed Mister Ramahi, it started a chain reaction severely weakening the few followers his family still had. There are none left now. Whatever caused the explosion at the Catalyst is unknown to me. Ah. We have finished our tea. Charles, Bell, can you help Del?"

We heard Freesia, who had come down the stairs and stood on the bottom step and pleaded with sad cat eyes. *"And me too, please?"*

Bell and I were deep in thought on the drive back to my Pleasure Point home and didn't talk until we got in the house and poured ourselves a couple of glasses of Cabernet. We plopped down on the couch. It was after 5 pm, and the Winter sun was already setting. We let out a collective sigh.

"Well, Charles, what have we gotten into this time? Here I thought we'd just hang out, read, write, eat good food…" Bell gave me one of her sexy looks. "…and make love."

"Ooo. You tempt me, lover. But, yeah, I know. We were supposed to take it easy. Relax. However, I do have to go to work at Stor-Tech tomorrow morning. I don't want to give my supervisor another reason to yell at me. Of course, she will anyway."

"I don't know why you keep working there. That Denise makes it such a dysfunctional environment. Also, it's such a long commute."

"I know, love. But the pay is good."

"But, dear, you don't have to work. Because of my mother's investments, I now have enough money in my accounts to last us the rest of our lives. And someday, you'll…"

"Oh, you know me. I don't want to rely solely on your inheritance, or even my future inheritance, which, who knows, Granny could be around another eighty years or more and use it all up."

"But I love having you around. I wish you'd quit and just stay home and write."

"Oh, I will one of these days. I do want to write that novel that's been bouncing around in the back of my mind. Well… really, for now, I do like my work. I even like tech writing. I like getting a paycheck too. And, besides, I am investing almost half of it for our future. Oh, by the way, I saw the company president the other day, and I looked into his eyes. You know what I saw?"

"What? What?"

"Denise is going to be on her way out. Work should get more pleasant real soon. I also saw something else in his eyes about the company, and…."

The phone rang interrupting our conversation. I picked it up. "Hello?"

"Hello…Ch… Charles B… Blue? This… this is Del… Del Prentiss." His voice sounded weak, as if he'd been crying. "Ma… Madam Seren said I should… call you. You pro… probably don't remember me. It's b… been a long time."

"Yes, it has been. And, yes, Del, I remember you. You were the only talented member of that old band you were in. You also seemed nicer than the rest of those guys."

"Thank you, Charles. I'm really s… sorry to bo… bother you. I really d… don't want to ta… talk about th… this over the ph… phone. Can I come over? Is it okay? Madam Seren said you a… agreed to he… help."

"Of course you can come over. And I'm really sorry about your loss."

"Th… thank you. Where d… do you live?"

I gave him our address and directions. Del said he lived in the Seabright district and could be here in fifteen minutes.

"Bell, when he drives up, we need to lower our house protection spell."

"I'll make some coffee."

Del didn't drive up. He was riding a bicycle and arrived in exactly fifteen minutes. His bike looked like one of those new mountain-style bikes with fat knobby tires. He turned off the small headlight fastened to his handlebars. Bell and I lowered our protection spell while he locked his bike to our mailbox post and took off his riding helmet. Even though it was a chilly December evening, Del was wearing shorts. His legs were muscular and looked as if he biked a lot.

"Del. Please come in. Let me introduce you to my best friend here, Bell. Bell, meet Del."

"I'm pleased to meet you, Del. I'm sorry it's under such dire circumstances."

Del could barely speak. I could see he was nervous and choked up. His eyes were red, either from crying or lack of sleep… or both. It was hard to tell. I could not read his eyes, which was often the case with others with abilities, even a minimal one like Del's. I seemed to sense something else in him but couldn't put my finger on it. He had a large bandage over his right eye. I held onto my medicine bag, the one my grandfather, Peter Red Feather had left for me, and recited an Ohlone healing spell to ease Del's mind. He took a deep breath and was able to speak clearly.

"I'm really sorry to disturb you. Madam Seren spoke very highly of both of you and said you might be able to help me find out what happened to my son."

"I really hope we can."

Bell asked, "Is there anything you can tell us about what happened?"

"I was being escorted out by the Catalyst's security guard and about to leave when we were knocked down when the back door was blasted open. The door hit me and cut my forehead here. Ten stitches." He pointed to the bandage. "When I jumped up and ran out, I saw a very bright light had engulfed my son's VW bus and turned it into a pile of ashes. The light disappeared and the hot white flame was… gone. Marty… was… gone…. I mean… no body. No… ashes. Gone."

Del was choking up again. I held my medicine bag and eased his mind. "I'm sorry I break down so easily. I wish I had more power, like the ones you two have, or even some of those odd powers of my old band mate, Pete Ramahi."

"Uh…" I started stuttering myself. I held onto my medicine bag to help center me. "Pete Ramahi is dead. I know you don't know this, but he and his mother killed my parents. Then years later he murdered several of my old friends to get at me. He then tried to kill me. He had also poisoned Bell here and put her into a twenty-year death sleep. He was bad news."

"Wow. I knew he had serious issues. I think he enchanted us somehow to do whatever he wanted. I didn't know how bad he was at the time. I did keep trying to calm him down, but his power was too much for me to deal with."

"Del, we know that Pete and his parents were practitioners of dark magic and tried to take over the local witch, warlock, and psychic communities. They always confronted those who opposed them, trying to destroy their abilities, and if they couldn't, they would kill them. My Granny fought back when Pete's father tried to attack her. He underestimated her abilities, and Pete's father died at her hand. That's why Pete and his mother went after me and my family and friends for revenge."

"I'm really sorry to hear that. That must be why Pete seldom came to rehearsals. Oh… Speaking of Pete. I just remembered. There was someone who showed up at gigs who appeared to have abilities a lot like Pete, maybe more. Maybe a Ramahi follower. Anyway, when the band broke up, Pete disappeared as well as that person he talked to. I never heard from him again."

Bell reached over and touched Del's shoulder and asked, "You said you thought he was a Ramahi follower. Can you remember what he looked like?"

"Not he, it was a she and unforgettable. She was very tall, maybe close to six feet, very thin and looked kind of emaciated, like she didn't eat well. Her complexion was pale. You'd think she was albino, but she had dark brown, almost black-looking eyes. I don't think she ever went out into the sun. Oh, and her hair was pure white, thick, and long, reaching past her waist. She wore very dark lipstick and a tight, black body suit with a black motorcycle jacket. Very goth looking. She looked older, but I think Pete had a thing for her."

"I don't recall anyone like that at the couple of gigs your band and mine played together. I'm sure she would have stood out. Now, Bell, don't look at me like that. You stand out too, love." Bell smiled at me.

"She never came to our day gigs, only our night ones. Say, you don't think she's a…"

"Vampire?" Bell questioned.

"That's what I felt at the time, but I don't know. There was something else about her. I sometimes felt I knew her from somewhere."

"Let me ask you this," I queried. "What are your abilities?"

"Very few. Really, only one, to make heavy things lighter. I had a few more when I was young but lost most of them. My father, Ifan, was Celtic. Welsh. Our family in the old country go back many centuries in the area known as Snowdon. Many of the old stone circles in that part of Wales were warlock and witch gathering places and burial sites. Unfortunately, I didn't inherit much from my old relations or my father. My mother, Tegan, was also Welsh but lived in New York. She left when I was four. I don't really remember her. Father said she was a mortal, but I understood she knew quite a lot about our kind. Dad told me when he met her, she had a job as an investigative reporter for a publisher who put out tabloids, like the Star or Enquirer. My father said he fell for her and helped her by reciting outlandish warlock stories. He said the publisher ate it up.

"Unfortunately, those stories were read by some who got extremely upset and came after my mother. My father never found out who it was and where mother went. My father always missed her. He passed away last year. Now I want to find out what happened to my... mother, my... my wife, and n...now my... my son."

Chapter 3

Del's despondency and hesitance returned. Once again, I used my medicine bag to ease his mind. He continued.

"I was told by Madam Seren that you both have very strong abilities. I… I could really use your help. Can I count on you?"

Bell answered for both of us. "Yes. We told Gwyn… Madam Seren, that we would. Now, we understand this… problem occurred in the parking lot behind the Catalyst. Yes? Okay, then, Charles and I will start by looking there."

"I… I don't think I can ever go back there again."

"You don't have to," I said. "We'll probably be there a while poking around and trying to get a feel for the…. No, you don't have to go. But give us your phone number so we can contact you. Here." I picked up my small address book and a pencil off my desk and handed it to Del. He wrote down his address and phone number.

"I'm sorry to take up so much of your time. It's late, and you probably want to have dinner. I should be going."

"Don't worry." Bell put her hand on his shoulder. "Whatever happened could possibly be a threat to all of us. We'll help the best we can."

Del thanked us, shook our hands and left. We watched him unlock his bike, put on his helmet, and ride off. Bell and I stood there in silence for a minute with our arms around each other. Bell broke the silence.

"We should get over to the Catalyst right now before the evidence, if there is any, is contaminated or destroyed."

The five-mile drive from Pleasure Point to downtown Santa Cruz usually took less than fifteen minutes, but because of some nighttime road work, traffic was backed up. It took us nearly 45 minutes to get to the parking lot behind the Catalyst, which was full, so we ended up parking on Cedar Street a half block away. It was after seven.

"Damn. I don't have any change for the parking meter. Do you have any Bell?"

"No, but I have this." Bell touched the coin slot on the parking meter, said a few words and turned the handle. "Okay, we now have two hours to look around."

"Thanks, Bell. You're amazing. You've got to teach me to do that one of these days. Okay. Let's go see what we can see."

We walked hand in hand to the parking lot behind the Catalyst. It was well lit. A tour bus was parked next to the back wall and some roadies were unloading equipment from it. Behind the bus was some pavement that looked like it had melted then hardened again. It had a small dip in it. There were still a few shards of glass in the dip that twinkled in the light.

"Crud," I said. "This has been driven over too many times. Well, let's touch it and try to get a feel of whatever happened here."

We squatted down across from each other and put our right hands down in the side of the dip. We closed our eyes and recited a short incantation. I spoke in Romani; Bell spoke in English.

Nothing.

"Bell, it's no use. This is too old and too many cars and people have driven or walked over this."

"Let me try one more thing, Charles." Bell stood in the middle of the dip and closed her eyes and again recited another incantation. "Bright light. That's all I can see. Just like Madam Seren said. It seems to have come from... that church over there across the street." She pointed. "The Elm Street Mission."

The two roadies who were unloading the bus were taking a break and sharing what was obviously a joint, its tip glowing as they toked. They had been staring at us while we were touching the pavement. We waved. They laughed and waved back. A few seconds later a familiar guy came out the repaired back door of the Catalyst and angrily said something to the roadies. One of them pinched the end of the roach and put it in a small tin that he put in his coat pocket. The other laughed and gave the guy the finger. They both shook their heads and went back to work.

"Well, that was interesting. I think that guy was Warren Zevon. Must be playing here tonight."

Bell shrugged. "Who's Warren Zevon? Someone you played

with?"

"Nah. He's just another popular recording artist." I turned to look at the church. "Okay, Bell, let's go across the street and check out that place."

We walked up a couple of steps to the front door of the Elm Street Mission. A single light bulb dangling from a wire lit the landing where we stood. We tried the door, but it was locked. Bell touched the door and was thinking of opening it with an incantation but decided against it. "Some lights are on, and it's still warm in there. I sense no one is inside. They must have left recently. I don't sense anything out of the ordinary... except..."

"Except this note pinned to the door. Kinda cryptic. 'Volcano. Retreat.' Hmm. A warning?"

I could see that Bell was running different ideas through her mind. "I'm pretty sure it's a place."

My stomach growled.

"Uh... Bell, we missed dinner. I'm hungry. We still have more than an hour on our parking meter. Let's walk over to the food tent and see what's available."

There were six large arched tent-like temporary buildings set up in three parking lots along Cedar Street two blocks from the Catalyst. Many of the stores and restaurants displaced by the '89 earthquake were able to keep open in the tents. One of the busiest was Bookshop Santa Cruz, my favorite independent bookstore. They had one whole tent for the large inventory they salvaged from their collapsed storefront. The other busy tent housed the food court. There were several different restaurants and beverage counters.

We gravitated to the best smelling counter, India Joze. Bell ordered gado gado, a warm garlicky Indonesian-style salad with a peanut sauce and tofu, and I got some sautéed local calamari, also garlicky, with snow peas. It took a little while to be prepared, but it was worth it. We grabbed a couple of glasses of a cool chardonnay from another booth and sat down at a table to dig in. Delicious.

The food tent was noisy, so we didn't talk much while eating. With the cacophony of voices and recorded music reverberating through the building, it was hard to talk out loud or telepathically. I tried talking both ways. Bell smiled at me and shrugged.

After we finished our meals and wine, we headed back to our van. Twenty minutes later, with traffic back to normal, we pulled into the driveway of my Pleasure Point home.

"Uh… Bell, did we leave the lights on? Jeez. Look. The front door is open. We did reinstall the protection spell after Del left, didn't we?"

"We did. I'm sure of it. It has to be someone with power. Hey! I see movement. Someone is coming out. We better protect… Uh… Hey! It's Yana!"

"Granny?"

We jumped out of the van and Granny gave us both hugs.

"So sorry to surprise you, dear ones. I was gazing into my old, cracked crystal and got a bad feeling. I looked harder and all I could see was a bright light and some church."

"Could you see the name of the church, Granny?"

"I could only make out one word, Mission, and I felt it was the Santa Cruz Mission. I decided to come down from the City to see if you knew about it."

"Bell and I were just there a couple of hours ago. It's not the Santa Cruz Mission, it's the Elm Street Mission. It's some holy roller type of church downtown. And, yes, we were there checking out where young Marty Prentiss's VW bus burned up. You heard about that? Yeah? Okay. Uh… we didn't see a car. How did you get here?"

"Oh…" She paused, then continued. "Well, I got a lift. And… no, I wasn't hitchhiking. Those days are far behind me. Never mind now, I'll tell you later. Yes, the Elm Street Mission. That makes more sense. And Prentiss. I know that name. I seem to remember a young warlock named Prentiss who came into the Mystic Eye one time. I had a feeling he didn't have many powers. He was looking through the books to see about learning more. Bell, you might have even waited on him. Or was it your mother.? So hard to remember back that far."

"It must have been you or Mother," Bell replied. "Del was here yesterday asking us to look into his son's disappearance."

"Delwood! That was his name. Yes. I did wait on him. Charles, you still have my notebooks? The ones from, maybe, 1969 through 1970, with the Mystic Eye sales and visits?"

"Of course, Granny. I brought them here while our Victorian is being restored and remodeled. Uh… how is it going with the work there?"

"It's coming along. The basement has the new plumbing and electricity in and space for a washer and dryer where your shop used to be. The electrical contractor is still rewiring the entire house."

"What about my tenants? Are they okay with all the work

going on?"

"I didn't want them and their children to be uncomfortable, so I put them up in a nice motor hotel in Cow Hollow. I'm even paying for their restaurant meals."

"That's sweet of you, Yana. Charles, pull out those sales notebooks"

I went into the bedroom and opened a large old leather covered steamer trunk; one I picked up at a local yard sale maybe five years ago. It normally looked empty. I closed my eyes, recited an unprotecting spell, opened the trunk and all the notebooks were there. I thumbed through them and pulled out the two sales notebooks with the dates Granny suggested and brought them into the living room.

"Here, Granny. I think one of these might have what you're looking for."

"Thank you, dear. Let us see. I'm trying to remember… maybe…" Granny thumbed through the first one "Ah. Here he is. He came in when we were having a solstice holiday sale. It shows here that he only bought some herbal tea. No books. Ah, here's a note I wrote on the back of the sales receipt. Yes. I was curious about what he said. He was taking the tea to his uncle in… odd… Volcano."

Bell and I looked at each other with questioning eyes.

"Children, I see you're concerned about something."

"Granny, there was a note on the door of that Elm Street Mission that had two words on it: Volcano. Retreat. So, it must be a place. I wonder where it is?"

"Maybe we can find something about it at the bookstore or library."

Granny put her hand on mine. "Or, dear, I can call Garrett. His mind is a storehouse of knowledge."

Garrett Stone was one of Granny's oldest friends and was going to sell his house to her because he planned to leave for England to live there and take care of his ailing older brother. Granny grabbed the phone and dialed Garrett's number.

He answered on the first ring. "Hello, Yana." Granny said hello back. Garrett often knew who was calling, even before his phone would ring. "It is an honor to hear your voice again. I sense you have a question. About my house?"

"No. Not now, Garrett. I would rather talk to you about that in person. The reason I'm calling, dear Garrett, is to pick your brain. You do have an encyclopedic memory."

Garrett laughed. "Funny. When I was young and in grade school, some of the so-called cool kids called me Britannica brain, because I could answer any question about anything. I read a lot. I have a photographic memory."

"Well, see if your photographic memory can tell us about some place in California called Volcano."

"Well, yes. Volcano, California. The town is named for its setting in a bowl-shaped valley that early miners thought was caused by a volcano. It was not of course. It is in Amador County, fifteen miles northeast of Sutter Creek off of highway 49, also known as the Gold Chain Highway."

"Garrett, dear, you are wonderful. I think we're going to have to go there for a day or two to look around."

"You will see that Volcano is a little out of the way. Many go there to visit the caves, which I need to warn you about."

"I think I know. Is one of them the Black Chasm Cavern?"

"Yes, it is, Yana. How did you know that?"

"My ex-husband, Peter Red Feather, told me the story he heard from other Indians about that cave and the Masonic cave that is close by there. Even some of the other caves in the gold rush country are supposed to cause problems for our kind. They sap your strength, and you can't get it back. Or so they say."

"Oh, yes. That is the story I have heard too. You know, I do not know if all that is true, but if you go to Volcano, it is wise to be cautious around those caves."

Chapter 4

Granny thanked Garrett and hung up. She was quiet and stared off into space for a few minutes as if she was thinking about the past. Bell cleared her throat waking Granny from her reverie. She shrugged.

"Sorry, children, I was deep in thought. Charles, can you contact Mister Prentiss? Delwood? I would like to find out who his uncle in Volcano is before we drive there."

"I'll do that. Granny, do we need to drive you to San Francisco on the way so you can pack?"

"No, dear, I'm good. I brought my satchel with a few things. But you can take me to a drug store later so I can pick up a little something more for the trip."

I went out to the van and grabbed the California road map out of the glove box and brought it into the house. I spread it out on the dining table.

"Let's see. Okay, here's highway 49. You said Garrett told you it was east... northeast of Sutter Creek. Ah... here it is. And... that little dot over here is Volcano. Tiny place. It looks like it will take four or five hours to get there. Some twisty roads. Too bad we can't take the Miata. Oh well, the van will be more comfortable for the three of us."

Bell put her hand on my shoulder. "Better call Del."

I grabbed my small address book off of my desk and dialed his number.

Del didn't answer, but a girl who sounded young and with a shaky voice answered. I sensed she had been crying.

"Hello. This is Charles Blue. Is Del there?"

"He..." She sniffed. "Daddy's not here. He... he went to the store."

"I'm sorry to bother you, but do you know when he'll be back?"

"I..." She sniffed again. "I don't know. Daddy is..." Sniff. "...Daddy didn't say."

"Well, when he returns, have him call me. It's very important. Thank you. And, again, I'm sorry."

She hung up without saying anything else.

Del didn't get back to me that day. Later the next morning after breakfast I dialed his number again. This time a man answered, but it was not Del. "Yeah! What do you want! Whatever it is! We're! Not! Buying! Fuck off!"

He hung up.

I turned to Bell and Granny. "Some real jerk answered, and he didn't even let me ask about Del. He just yelled, swore, and hung up! Bell, I think we should go over to Del's house and see if he's there at all. I didn't like the feeling I got from that guy who answered the phone."

"I got a weird buzz in my head from that call too. You're right. We need to go there and see for ourselves if Del is there… or wherever he might be."

"Crud. I'd better call work first and say I won't be in today."

I dialed Denise's number at Stor-Tech. "Hi Denise. I'm afraid I won't be able to come in today. There's a family emergency I must take care of." Tiny lie. A family of witches and warlocks.

"Okay. Take all the time you need. Goodbye."

I hung up, surprised. "Jeez, Bell. Denise sounded odd. She didn't yell at me. Just told me to take all the time I needed. Maybe she already knows she's getting laid off."

I reached over and grabbed my little address book and found the one Del wrote down. It was 211 1st Avenue. Once again, I ran out to the van and grabbed another map. This one for Santa Cruz. I spread it out on the table for us to find Del's street.

"One block off of Seabright. Not that far. Should be easy to find."

"Let's go, Charles. Keep your medicine bag ready, just in case."

"Be careful, my dears." Granny looked worried.

Del's house was in the middle of the block among beautiful homes with well-manicured yards. His house was different. It looked a little newer and not much bigger than mine but in worse shape. Paint was peeling from the wood siding and the front window was cracked. The grass was long. Even with the two days of rain we had last week, the lawn was brown. Dandelion weeds were scattered throughout the grass, some still flowering but most had gone to puffy seed. Quite a contrast to the other homes on the block.

There was one car in the driveway and another parked on the lawn next to it. A third was in the street in front of the house. All three cars were expensive looking and foreign. The two in and by the driveway were brand new Mercedes sedans, one white and one black. They both still had the temporary paper plates from the car dealer. The third car, on the street, was a black two-seater, Porsche 911, also with a paper plate. I parked behind it.

"Maybe these people are relatives, here for a memorial for Marty or something," Bell said. "Something odd about all these brand-new cars."

"Those cars aren't cheap," I replied. "Jeez. If they have money, you think they'd hire a gardener for Del… and a painter. That house needs work."

Bell and I got out of our van, walked up to the front door and pressed the button to ring the doorbell. I didn't hear the bell ring, so I started to knock. But before I could, the door swung open hard. We heard it hit the wall with a loud bang. An elderly man looked at us with a scowl. He was a little shorter than me and had long gray hair tied back in a ponytail. He was clean shaven and dressed in a black t-shirt tucked into black jeans. He was barefoot.

"What the fuck do you want? Get out!"

I looked into his eyes and saw a totally dysfunctional and confrontational character. No powers of any kind, but I did get the feeling he seemed to have an understanding of them. He started to close the door on us, so I decided to touch my medicine bag and try to calm him enough for us to get in. It worked. He opened the door wider and motioned for us to come in. He still didn't smile though.

"Thank you for your warm welcome," I said sarcastically. Even though it was foggy and chilly outside, he left the door open as he led us into the living room. I glanced back and saw that the doorknob had nearly gone through the sheetrock wall when he opened the door so violently.

In the living room were two very well-dressed couples and a woman dressed identical to the guy who let us in. Her hair was also long and gray and her ponytail was tied back so tight it stretched the wrinkles out of her pudgy face. Her t-shirt and black jeans clung to her overweight body like a second skin. The guy who let us in sat down beside her. She had a scowl that matched his. No one said hello. They all had mixed drinks in their hands. It wasn't even noon yet. They all looked at us like we were bothering them. I quickly scanned their eyes. Dysfunctional. Entitlement. Greed. Nothing.

Nothing? I could not read the eyes of a couple sitting in the corner. Both short and also dressed in black. Odd, too, a young blond girl sitting with a young man turned her head before I could read her eyes. Everyone had their shoes off.

There were two guitars, a Fender Stratocaster and a Gibson bass, laying on the floor, obviously knocked off their stands by someone in this crowd. The Fender's neck looked broken. I felt anger.

I gritted my teeth and introduced Bell and myself to them. No reciprocation. They were quiet and staring. They all scowled... and sipped their drinks. Okay. I spoke to Bell telepathically. *"I think it's time for a little incantation to get these weirdos to talk."*

"How about this?"

Bell casually raised her hand, palm facing the group, and quietly mouthed an incantation. We started hearing their thoughts. Actually, only the thoughts of three of them. Odd again.

"Who are those..." "They don't belong..." "What the fu..." "Why isn't Del here..." "I don't feel good..." "Damn it all, my drink's too watery..."

Finally, I asked, "Where is Del? We came to see him."

The man in black who let us in finally spoke. "We're waiting for the... uh, him. He was not here when we arrived. So, you can leave now. We're in fucking mourning here."

No, they weren't. I could see that in his eyes. What I couldn't see was why they were here. I also got nothing from that other couple or from the young girl with their son. She kept looking away. I again spoke to Bell telepathically. *"Let's get out of this loony bin. We need to find Del."*

We didn't say goodbye and just walked out the open front door. It was loudly slammed shut as we reached our van. Before we got in, we could hear voices loudly arguing with each other through the cracked window.

"Bell, hear that? They're arguing about us... and cursing Del."

"Sounds like they suspect us and him of being... hear that? Special. Probably because we asked about Del. I wonder what they're all hanging around for? I couldn't see that in their eyes."

"I couldn't see that either. Come on. Let's get back home and tell Granny. Look! That old gray-haired guy's looking at us through the window." I forced a smile and waved, and he yanked the curtains closed. "Yeah. That guy does think we're... well, what we are."

About ten minutes later I pulled into my driveway. As we got out of the van, Granny rushed out to us waving a piece of notepaper.

"Charles, dear, Del called while you were gone. He wants to talk to you right away. He made it sound terribly urgent. Here is his number."

Bell and I hurried inside, and I immediately picked up the phone and dialed. Del picked up on the first ring.

"Del. Charles here. Are you okay?"

"Under the circumstances, I'm okay. I'm with my Uncle Dean in Volcano. My daughter, Dria, is with us too."

"We were awfully worried about you so we stopped by your house. It was full of strange people. I used a little incantation to get invited in, but only the older guy spoke. He swore a lot. Everyone else was deathly silent."

"That's why we left. I saw them starting to arrive after I got back from the store. Dria and I grabbed what we could and snuck out into the back alley where I kept my old Ford van and drove here. Anyway, two of them claim to be related to my mother's side of the family. I doubt it. They showed up only once before when I was little. Anyway, for some reason, they think my mom hid something with me—something that may be special to them… like money. That older couple who look alike are actually twin brother and sister. Jerry and Terry Wheeler. They've lived together their whole life in a weird incestuous relationship. I'm sure their surviving half-wit son, Nicolas, is there with his current girlfriend. I don't know her name or who the other couple are. They're not relations but must be followers of the Wheelers. I never liked them. They're foul-mouthed alcoholics."

"Yeah. We noticed they all had drinks in their hands. Liquid lunch, it looked like. The couple you don't know, their presence seemed odd to Bell and me."

"I've no idea who they are. I didn't see them arrive."

"Del, why are you in Volcano?"

"My uncle's old place here has always been a sanctuary for me and my kids. By the way, you'll be surprised by my Uncle Dean. He is a very good wizard."

"Wizard? Not a warlock?"

"Wizard. He may be the last of his kind. Yes, he has a knack for real magic. Not the stage rabbit-out-of-the-hat kind. The real stuff. He moved to Volcano around the time I was born to get away from my mom's so-called family."

"You mean those who are in your house right now?"

"Yes. Those and some of their old cult. He had run ins with them in the distant past. That odd couple you said was at my house may have joined that cult."

"Cult? The Wheelers have a cult?"

"Yes. A fake fundamentalist Christian cult. It started when they were much younger, and they used donations from their flock to fund what they called ministry work... well, really it was witch hunt work. They found out about dad's and Uncle Dean's abilities nearly forty years ago and wanted to stamp them out. Said they were the devil's spawn and blamed them both for my mother's disappearance. They found others who had the same witch hunt philosophy, and they all worked together to eradicate our kind. Fortunately, Dad and Uncle Dean were able to avoid them."

"Is the cult still active?"

"Hard to say. I don't think they have many followers. Maybe just that one weird couple now. Dad had told me when I was old enough to understand that nearly all of their old cult members disappeared, probably killed, during a botched raid on an evil family. Yes, Charles, it was the Ramahi family. The thing is, as my dad told me, the Wheelers never went on any of the raids. They always delegated that to the peasants, as they so often called their followers. So, they survived with all the money they collected from their members."

"Del, the way old Jerry Wheeler swore, he sure didn't sound like a fundamentalist Christian."

"I know. The Wheelers only used that as a premise to con money from their rich flock."

Bell telepathed to me to ask Del about the cars. "Del, all three couples at your house have brand new expensive foreign cars. Do they still have a lot of their cult money?"

"I really don't know. Last I heard, the Wheelers blew all the money they had in Vegas. So, maybe they've restarted the cult and are getting more donations. Uncle Dean isn't sure either when I asked him. Now. The main reason I called. Can you and Bell come here to Volcano? There's a nice old hotel here, called the Saint George. It may be a little busy with Christmas coming up, but Uncle Dean said he can use his magic to make sure some rooms are available for you. Your grandmother is welcome too. I think she'd have a nice time talking to Uncle Dean."

Chapter 5

After Del and I said our goodbyes, I looked over to Bell and Granny. They were staring at me with curious looks on their faces.

"So, you feel like a road trip?"

"Volcano?" Bell and Granny both said at the same time.

"Yep. When do you want to go? Tomorrow? Good. I'll call Del back to let him know."

"Charles, love, tell Del about the note on the door of the Elm Street Mission too."

I did. Del said he'd look to see if there were any new check-ins at both hotels in town and if a retreat of some kind was happening. But he wanted to walk over to the Saint George and book two rooms for us first. He told us the hotel had a restaurant in it that had decent food. He also said after we get settled in, his uncle would like to invite us to dinner at his home.

Granny had told me earlier she needed to get a few items at the drug store, so that afternoon I drove her to Horsnyder Pharmacy on the Eastside of Santa Cruz.

When we got out of the van, I asked Granny, "So, what do you need here? Do you need a prescription filled?"

"Oh, heavens no, dear Charles. I don't take any prescription medicines. I do need a new toothbrush and toothpaste since I forgot to pack mine. We also need to get some items for protection."

"Protection? From what. Making babies?"

Granny smiled, then got serious. "Charles. Dear, dear Charles. Protection for caves. Remember, I told you caves may not be good for our kind. Being close to, or inside a cave may lessen our strength. I've heard it said it may even take powers totally away, and that the 'breath of the earth' can affect witches and warlocks. Del's uncle is a wizard. He might not be affected at all. I'm sure he has lived in that area for a long time."

"But Granny, when we were in the caves under Telegraph Hill, our powers weren't lessened."

"Those were man-made caves. Anything man-made, like the mines in the gold rush country, are safe for us. Natural caves are another story."

So, Granny, what protection do we need to pick up?" I grabbed a shopping basket.

"Let's look around." We started walking up and down each aisle. "Okay. I'm sure we need these face masks like the doctors wear. Let's see. What else?" We came across a young male clerk in a wrinkled store smock and long curly hair that looked like it needed washing. He was stocking adult diapers on a shelf in front of us. Granny asked him, "Young man, can you tell me where the sunscreen is?"

He answered. Sort of. "It's the wrong time of year... uh, mam. We get big shipments in the late spring. Oh. You need some now? For sure. Aisle 4 on the end by the pharmacy are all we have right now."

Granny thanked him. He replied, "No problem," and went on with his shelf stocking.

Granny stared at him. I could see a little anger in her face. Her teeth clenched. She spoke to me telepathically. *"Why can't these young people learn to say 'you're welcome' instead of 'no problem'"* She used air quotes twice, then once more. *"Is it usually a 'problem' for them to wait on us?"*

I didn't know how to reply to that. I think Granny was just venting anyway. "Granny, there's the sunscreen. What kind do you need?"

She took a deep breath to center and calm herself. "Find one with the highest SPF rating. See if there's a large container that's SPF 50 or more."

The clerk made it sound like the drug store barely had any sunscreen. There were two full shelves with several brands, fragrances, mostly cocoanut, and sizes. It took a few minutes, but I found what Granny wanted.

"Anything else?"

"One more thing. A gallon of purified water."

We came to the last aisle. No purified water. They only had small bottles of spring water along with sodas in a refrigerated case. "Granny, I think we'll have to stop at Shopper's Corner for that."

We stopped there, picked up the water, and drove back to the house.

Before we got out of the van, I had a question for Granny. "Do you remember Madam Seren? Gwyn?"

"Why, yes dear. I haven't seen her for a long time. Is she here in Santa Cruz?"

"Yes, she is. She lives on a boat at the yacht harbor. She lives with a talking cat."

"I beg your pardon. Talking cat?"

"Well, she talks telepathically. She was transformed from her human self by Pete Ramahi's mother. I wanted to ask you if you know a way to bring her back."

"Ah. I'll have to look through my notes. I have a feeling it might take the three of us to counter the old Ramahi curse and pull her back to human form. I would like to see Gwyn again. I like her."

"Maybe we can go over to her boat after we get back. Let's go in."

I carried Granny's purchases in and set them on the kitchen table. Bell was in the bedroom packing her small suitcase. She looked up when Granny and I came in.

"Charles, how long do you think we'll be in Volcano? I want to make sure I have enough clothes and stuff."

"Hopefully no more than a couple of days, but, just in case, pack for a week. Now, where did I put my backpack?"

"Where you left it when we moved in here, silly. Back of the closet."

Sure enough. Right behind the clothes hamper. I've had that backpack since college when I carried all my textbooks, notebooks, and lunch in it. It was well-worn and nearly as large as Bell's suitcase and Granny's carpet bag. I pulled it out of the closet and set it on the bed and started to pack.

By ten the next morning we had loaded our van and were ready to start our drive to Volcano. I thought I had better call work again to remind Denise that I wouldn't be in for the rest of the week. I didn't get Denise. I got one of my work buddies.

"Fred. Hi. I thought this was Denise's number."

"Hey, buddy, you'll be happy to know that she got fired yesterday. The president found out about her lack of tech knowledge and her bitchy attitude. The wicked witch is dead. She's melted! She's melted! Ha. Oh, hey buddy, I've been asked to supervise our department temporarily. Got a little raise too. Huzzah!"

"That's great Fred. You deserve it. Hey, guy, I called because I won't be in for several days, possibly the week. There's been a death..." How should I put this? "...in the family." I didn't mind fibbing to Denise, but I felt a little guilty fibbing to Fred.

"Oh. Sorry to hear that. Take all the time you need. There's not much happening here anyway. Where are you heading, anyway?"

Might as well tell him. "A little old mining town up in the gold rush country called Volcano."

"Volcano? Never heard of it. Is there a volcano there?"

"Nope. I heard it's some bowl-shaped valley that miners back in the old days thought was formed by a volcano, so they named the town Volcano. There's several natural caves there besides all the mines."

"Ooo. I like exploring caves. I'll have to check it out some day. Hey, buddy, take care. Drive carefully. See you when you get back."

I thanked him and hung up.

"Okay, Bell, Granny, let's go."

Four hours later, we arrived in Volcano and parked in front of the St. George Hotel.

Looking around, we could see that it was a pretty small town nestled in a small valley with oak trees along the streets and fir and pine trees at the higher elevations above town. The three-story hotel was on the main street and was obviously the largest building there. Attached to one side of the hotel was an old-time saloon. I was looking forward to checking it out and having a drink.

A sign in front of the hotel said it was on the National Register of Historic Places and gave a very short history of the building. It was originally built in 1852 as a boarding house. The current St. George Hotel was built in 1867 of brick after the wooden boarding house and subsequent hotels burned three times. Cool history, I thought.

It might be too early to check in, but I wanted to go into the lobby and ask. No one was at the desk, so I rang the small push bell on the counter. A short and slightly overweight elderly lady in an old-fashioned western floor-length gingham dress came in through a door that must have been the office. Her hair was salt and pepper, more salt than pepper, and tied up in a bun. Her cheerful smile raised her puffy cheeks and looked genuine, not put on for customers. I could see she was a happy person.

"Good afternoon," she said with a Southern-sounding drawl. "You must be the Blue party. Dean's nice nephew said you were coming today. Yes, I have two lovely rooms in the annex building in back all ready for you."

I asked, "How much do we owe you for the rooms?"

"No worries, dear. It's paid for by our old friend Dean Prentiss. He wanted me to let him know when you got here. Mister Blue, please sign the register."

I did and she handed us our keys and pointed to the back door. "You're in the Jerome and National rooms in the annex. Right through that door and across the patio."

Bell and I went back to the van and got our luggage and bags and caught up to Granny who was already entering the Jerome room. I followed her in and set her carpet bag on a suitcase rack and her bag of items she got at the pharmacy and grocery store on top of the chest of drawers. Her room looked comfortable in an antique-looking way.

She sat down in an easy chair and let out a sigh. "I need to rest up a bit after that long drive before our evening with Del and his uncle Dean. I might even take a little nap."

"I can use my medicine bag to help you."

"No, dear, not now. You and Bell go get settled in. I know you want to explore the town a little. Be sure not to get close to any caves on the outskirts of town."

I left Granny and went down the wooden porch to our room next door. The door had a carved wood sign on it saying National. Bell had put her suitcase on a folding stand. I dropped my backpack on the floor next to it. Like Granny's room, it was not large. It had a queen size mattress on a Victorian-style oak bedframe with a tall oak headboard. There were side tables and lamps on each side, a short three-drawer dresser, a small closet, and an easy chair in the corner. The front window looked out over a lovely garden with brick paths and a patio that had a couple of picnic tables in the middle of it. A side door led to a full-size bathroom with a tub and shower.

"Bell, love, you want to take a little walk around town? Might take, oh, ten minutes or so."

She laughed. "Yeah, it is a small town. I need to use the bathroom first."

"Me too. Maybe after our little walk we can get a drink in the ol' saloon."

I had tucked my thumbs in my belt and said it like a movie western cowboy, with a Texas drawl. Bell laughed and lightly punched me on the arm.

Volcano's Main Street was only a block long. After the hotel and bar, there was another bar that looked permanently closed, a convenience store called The Country Store, and a bakery. Around the corner on Consolation Street there was only one business, The Volcano Union Pub and Inn. The building looked a little run down, but the bar was open and looked busy.

We walked a little further up Consolation, enjoying some of the quaint old houses and cabins. Some of them still looked like they probably did when the mines were being worked in the mid 1800s. Two in a row were made of logs. One looked well maintained and had a white-washed picket fence around the front yard rose garden. The other didn't look lived in and most of the chinking was gone. You could see through the spaces between the logs. The front yard to that cabin was overgrown with tall grass and dry weeds and what looked like a bush of poison oak. As we walked by, we startled a young two-pronged buck that was nibbling the tall grass. We watched as it bound up the hill behind the cabin.

Then I started getting a tingling sensation. The matching griffin rings we both wore began to glow.

"Bell, do you feel that? Look at your ring."

"I do feel it. We better turn back. Maybe our rings are warning us of a cave… or something else."

With the town so small, we were back at the hotel bar within ten minutes. Several couples who looked like tourists filled the half dozen tables in the bar and a couple of tables in the adjoining restaurant. Two of them wore ugly green and red sweaters with large Rudolph the red nose reindeers on the front. Obviously here for the holidays. They were nursing beers and mixed drinks and munching on small bowls of salty peanuts. Half the twelve old wooden bar stools were occupied not with tourists, but older men who looked like regulars. Five of them had shot glasses they were filling from a whiskey bottle they kept passing between them. Only one was drinking beer. They all wore flannel shirts of various colors, tucked into jeans and denim coveralls. Three of them had long gray beards. Two others had five o'clock shadows—probably five o'clock last week. They were all laughing and joking around. The quiet one at the end of the bar, who was leaning over with his head in his hands, appeared clean shaven.

Bell and I sat down at two empty stools at the bar next to them. The guy next to me turned and said with whiskey tainted breath,

"Howdy strangers. Y'all from out of town? Visitin'?"

"Yeah," I answered. "We're here to visit a friend who's here with his uncle."

"Oh yeah? We probably know him if he lives here. Who is he?"

"His name is Dean Prentiss. We're supposed to have dinner at his place a little later."

"Dean. Yep. He's been here nearly as long as we all have. Odd bird, that one, but seems nice."

All the other guys at the bar overheard, and they smiled and nodded in agreement. A couple of them even said, "odd bird. Odd old bird."

The bartender, who looked a lot like the regulars, also with a long gray beard, asked what would we like. Bell asked for a glass of white wine, I asked for a pint of Sierra Nevada that was on tap.

The beer was refreshing. Bell said the cheap chablis that was poured from a box was awfully dry and a little like vinegar. She only took one sip and left the rest.

"Bell, we'd better go check on Granny and see if Del called about dinner yet."

"I'm calling now. Hello Charles. Hello Bell. Welcome to Volcano."

With all the talking going on in the bar and restaurant, we didn't hear Del walk in. He put his hands on both our backs when he spoke giving us a slight fright. When we saw who it was, Bell and I took deep breaths to settle ourselves and shook hands with him. He was smiling.

"Del." I said. "You're looking better than when we last saw you. You doing okay?"

"I am. My uncle Dean has a way of easing my mind. My

daughter, Dria, is doing better too. You will meet her and uncle Dean this evening. His home is easy to find. It's only a quarter mile up the road behind the Union Inn and Pub. His mailbox has a red-painted carved dragon on it. You can't miss it."

"What time should we be there?" Bell asked.

"You should come up by six before it gets too dark. I need to get back to see if Uncle Dean needs help with the preparations. See you in a couple of hours."

Del left. We had two hours before we had to get ready, so I ordered Bell a better glass of wine and we sat there drinking and taking in the ambience of the old bar.

Almost an hour later we said our goodbyes to the regulars who were still pouring and downing shots next to us. They all waved with their free hands.

We walked through the open door from the bar to the hotel and out the back to the annex building. I knocked on Granny's door. She opened it and we went in.

Granny asked, " Did Del or Dean call yet?"

"We just saw Del." I said. "He told us how to get to his uncle's place. We're to be there by six."

"Ah. Good. So, did you two have a nice walk?"

"Uh… yeah, until we got a few blocks away. Bell and I both felt a strange tingling sensation. Maybe a cave was in the area."

"Hopefully, Del's uncle's place isn't close to any. We really don't know where they are or how they can affect us. We might want to take precautions with some of the items I brought."

"I don't think that will be necessary Granny."

There was a knock on the door. I opened it.

"Hello. You must be Charles. And you two are Yana and Bell.

I'm Dean Prentiss." He was dressed similar to the guys in the bar. Flannel shirt tucked into jeans. He wore what looked like hiking boots. He was clean shaven but did have a short gray mustache. He didn't look very happy.

"I'm pleased to meet you. Are you okay?"

"I'm sorry, but we must postpone dinner tonight. Del and his daughter went for a walk and are missing."

Chapter 6

Dean Prentiss looked older than Granny, who has always looked the same age to me ever since she took me in some twenty-five years ago. I always figured she was in her eighties then and still looks it now. Granny invited him in. He didn't sit.

I asked, "Mister Prentiss. Dean. Do you have any idea what happened to Del?"

"I wish I knew. I do know that Del walked down to meet you."

"And we just saw him an hour ago."

"He came back and asked me if I needed help cooking. I did not, so he and Dria took a walk together before dinner. Through my wizard magic, I can locate family, no matter where they are in the world. I always know where they are. However, I lost track of them shortly after they left my place and headed up the road. Del said he wanted to show Dria the mines. Now my... magic can't locate them anywhere. After what happened to his son, I worry something might have happened to them too."

"Dean," Bell spoke. "Are there caves close by here? Charles and I got a strange feeling when we walked up the street past that Pub and Inn."

"There are none around this part of town. The closest large cave, Black Chasm, is a couple miles away. The smaller Masonic caves are a half mile to the south. You should… uh, not have had any cave feelings around town."

Granny asked, "Dean, we…" she motioned to Bell and me "have been told that our kind have a problem with caves. Was Del in one when he was younger?"

"His father… he thought that was how Del lost his warlock powers when he was in his teens. The two of them were visiting me. Del went exploring and wandered into the Masonic cave. I tried to use my magic to keep him out of the cave, but it was too late. The damage got… was done… uh, he lost all but one of his… uh, warlock powers. Del's own children grew up with the same one power. I really do not think he would ever go into one of those caves again."

"Interesting," I said. "Del didn't mention that . However, I get the feeling he didn't believe in it."

"Well, maybe. Del's mother… uh… did not have any witch abilities, but Del's father was a decent warlock. Del's children, Marty and Dria, being part warlock, never tried to increase their powers. They were too young and had other interests."

"Sounds like someone I know," Granny commented, looking at me. I shrugged and faked looking guilty and smiled.

"Well, anyway, Del developed a couple of very easy

incantations at first, but it only related to his music. As I said, he lost all but one in that cave. Marty picked up on the same one his dad had. Dria still has not tried to learn anything witch related and has not wanted to."

Granny put a hand on Dean's shoulder. "Dean, we can help look for Del and Dria if you want us to."

"Okay, if we have to look in the mines. I do not think they went the other direction to town. Sure. You can… uh, help."

Dean sounded reluctant.

Bell and I left Granny and Dean to get to know each other better. We walked over to the main hotel building and into the bar. The same guys were still sitting around. It looked like they were still passing the same bottle to each other, but it couldn't be. It looked fuller than before. Must be another bottle. Bell and I sat down on the same stools next to them.

The same guy next to us spoke. "Hello, strangers. New in town? Ya looks familiar." He slurred his words more than when we first met him. His whiskey breath was worse and nearly knocked me over.

"Yeah, pardner," I said, faking a western old-timer accent. "We were here meetin' ya just a while ago."

Bell kicked me under the bar and said telepathically, *"That's not nice, Charles. They might be offended if they sober up enough to remember you."*

"Sorry, Bell. I couldn't help myself."

Both of us heard a telepathic voice other than ours.

"Yeah, Charles. Bell is right. They will remember how you talked to them when they sober up."

The one guy at the other end of the bar nursing a beer was not with the five others sharing the whiskey bottle even though he'd been there as long. He looked similar to them, but he was clean shaven, and his hair was much shorter under his cowboy hat. He looked up and smiled at us.

"Garrett?" Bell and I said out loud.

The five regulars all turned to us and said together, "Wha?" Then went back to their drinking.

Back to telepathy. Garrett spoke first. "*I have been waiting here for you to get back. I am surprised you did not notice me sooner.*"

I had to chuckle. "Garrett, we didn't expect to see you here. And you blended in too well. We thought you were one of these local yokels."

"Yes, I guess I did. Even these inebriated old guys were thinking I was local."

"What brought you here to Volcano?"

"Research. After Yana asked me about this place, I had to check it out for myself. After all, I have only read about it. I wanted to experience it for a change."

"What kind of research?" Bell asked.

"The caves."

"Did you bring protection for going in them?"

"No. I really do not think that is necessary."

"But you might need it," I told Garrett. "It seems Del and his daughter have disappeared. We don't know if they're trapped in a mine or..."

"Or," Garrett cut in, "they were spirited away."

"Why do you say that? Are you suggesting Del and Dria could be dead?"

"Heavens no. They may have made a transference to a hidden realm just out of contact. That's something else I've read about. Or they may be in a mine or some other place that has quite a bit of iron ore in the walls."

Everything Garrett was relating wasn't making much sense to me and Bell, but coming from Garrett's photographic memory, it had to be so. We both had questioning looks on our faces.

Bell said, "We've never heard of any of this before. I don't think Yana knows about this either."

"Oh, I am sure Yana knows. Even with all the protection she brought, if we go into a mine that has iron ore, or even deep in a cavern, we will be out of contact to any of our kind until we emerge."

My turn to ask. "Wait a minute. You mentioned hidden realm. What is this?"

"That is hard to explain. I have not experienced it, but from my readings it has happened before. Ages ago. Some kind of device or talisman was used."

"Like our rings maybe? Both of ours glowed a few blocks from here." Bell pointed to hers.

"Your rings? My. I have never noticed those before. They are identical. Are they? What is that?" Garrett pointed to the amber stone on Bell's ring.

"It's a small piece of amber with a tiny insect embedded in it. Charles's ring has the same."

Garrett took Bell's hand and looked real close at the amber. "Ah. No wonder they occasionally glow. That is a lightning bug."

"Really? How can you tell?" I was staring at my own ring.

"Oh, etymology was just another of my many areas of research in the past. My old memory is still functioning quite well." Garrett chuckled, then got serious. "You know, your rings might give you the ability to *move through time and space. It is possible Del somehow did the same... or someone else made it possible."*

Granny walked into the bar. She had changed into an outfit similar to those worn by Garrett and the old timers at the bar. Red flannel shirt tucked into jeans. She even had on ankle-high brown hiking boots. She had a red bandanna tied around her gray hair that was now tied back in a ponytail.

"Granny!" I blurted out loud. The six old guys at the bar turned to look. Two of them wolf whistled. Granny smiled and blew them a kiss. Bell and I stared at her. So out of character. She came up and gave Garrett a tight hug.

"After Dean left I started to take a nap and suddenly had you on my mind. I knew you were here, Garrett, so I dressed for the occasion. You are here to help us find Del and Dria?"

"Not at first. But now, yes, Yana, I guess I can help."

I had to ask. "Uh... Granny, where did you get those clothes?"

"Out of my carpet bag, of course. I packed everything I'd need for this trip."

"But your bag is not that big? Or... Oh. Of course. A bottomless bag. Right?"

Granny came up and gave me a hug, pulled me down to her height and whispered in my ear. "Let us keep that to ourselves. Okay?"

"Okay, Granny. Sorry I blurted it out."

"No one caught what you said anyway. Garrett's talking to Bell, and those old miners at the bar are too busy drinking. Now, Charles dear, you and Bell need to go to your room and dress appropriately. We are going to meet Dean at his house in a half hour. Garrett?" Granny put her hand on his shoulder. "You want to go?"

Fifteen minutes later we were out the door and walking up Main Street. The sun had set an hour before, so I had pulled a flashlight out of my backpack before we left. We turned right on to Consolation. Barely fifty feet and just before the Volcano Union Pub and Inn was Emigrant Road, which ran diagonally off Consolation behind the pub. There was a slight incline heading up that road, and I could see Granny breathing heavy and beginning to slow down. I gave Bell my flashlight then held Granny's hand and used my other hand to hold onto my medicine bag. Granny breathed easier and was keeping up better.

About a hundred feet further, she pointed. "That is Dean's house there. It is the one with the carved dragon on the mailbox like he told me. Ah. There he is on the porch."

Dean was waving and motioning for us to come in. His house was old, probably from the gold rush days, but it had a shiny, new green metal roof. The exterior, a ship-lap wood siding, had a light stain that showed the natural wood. It was not a large house, but it looked big inside when we entered.

The living room was furnished with a full-sized sofa and a recliner upholstered in a tan leather. They faced a large fireplace made of river rock. Dean brought in an extra chair from his dining room. Once we all sat down, Dean clapped his hands once and the wood in the fireplace lit.

"It gets chilly here this time of year. This will make us more comfortable. Now. Who is this?" Dean closed his eyes and answered before I could make the introduction. "Garrett Stone. Ah. A good friend of Yana's. I know you will be a good friend to me too." He opened his eyes and looked at Garrett. "So glad to meet another of your kind." He pointed at Granny. "There are so few of you left. There are only two of my kind left."

Dean grew quiet for a few seconds before he continued. "Yes, you question that." Dean waved his hand. "Ah. Garrett. You have someone in your family who is a wizard... no, a wizardess."

"How did you know..." Garrett looked alarmed and glanced at Granny. She stared at him and had a questioning look in her eyes.

"Of the two wizards left in the world, there is only me and... Garrett, your half-sister is the only other of my kind left in the whole world. At least as far as I know."

"Garrett?" Granny said. "You never told me about her."

Garrett looked down at his feet, sighed, then looked up at Granny. "My sister... well, my half-sister, and I have the same mother. Her father was a wizard. Yes, Dean, his name was Dominic..."

"Dominic! Ah. A name from the past. He was a good man. Missed. Go on..."

"My father was a warlock, so I got his powers. My sister got her father's powers as a wizardess. We did not know of each other for over twenty years. We finally met at my mother's memorial service. That's when she told me her wizarding kind were almost extinct after her father passed away. She asked me not to tell anyone about her. She disappeared from my life as quickly as she came into it. Dean, I'm glad you told me she is still alive. Do you know where she is?"

"My... uh... magic has placed her in England. Some place called Dunwich."

"Dunwich!" Garrett exclaimed. "What a coincidence. My ailing brother, Henry, is there too. He moved there back in the 1930s. So odd. That is where I'll be moving in a few months, as you know, Yana. I've been reading a lot about that place. It is spelled D U N W I C H and is pronounced Dunnich. Sometimes called the Atlantis of England and the lost city. The port of Dunwich was larger, richer, and more important than London up to the 14th century. A series of severe storms caused massive erosion that caused most of the old city to fall into the sea. Oh… sorry. You know me, Yana, I get carried away with history. So, that is where my half-sister is."

Dean smiled at Garrett. "Now I remember who you are. Stoney! Britannica brain!" He laughed.

Garrett looked at Dean with a questioning sideways glance. "Uh…" Recognition. "Dippy?"

"Dippy?" Granny, Bell, and I questioned at the same time.

"That's what some of us at Marina Middle School called Dean at the time. Dean Prentiss. DP. Dippy. Dean, when was that? Ah… Eighth grade. So, so long ago."

Dean got serious again. "We can reminisce later, Stoney. We need to try to find Del and Dria. I felt their presence finally. But it is fleeting. Now I cannot. Well, it's too late to go look right now, so I think early tomorrow morning we should look in the first mine up the street. If we find nothing there, a half mile further is a second mine. Yana, it is a quarter mile up hill. Do you want to stay at the hotel?"

"No. I'll go too. My dear Charles can keep me going quite well."

Chapter 7

The next morning after a quick breakfast, the four of us met Dean back at his house. He was waiting on the porch, so we left right away and headed further up Emigrant Road. The December morning had warmed a little, but it was still chilly in the shade of the oak and pine trees along the way. I kept hold of Granny's hand with my other on my medicine bag. She was keeping up quite well on the steady incline.

As we walked along, Bell asked Dean the question I was about to ask. "Dean, why are we looking in a mine? This seems a little out of the way to try to find Del."

"Ah. I did not explain. Even when Del was small, he loved exploring the mines here. I even went with him back then to make sure he stayed safe. When he got older, I did not have to look out for him as much. He got to know some of these mines quite well.

When Del was here with his children, when they were young teens, he took them into the mines to show them around. Maybe Del took Dria into one again. I need to know if they got lost or trapped. The geologic makeup of those mines keeps my magic from locating them. Ah… there it is."

We had reached the hard-rock mine opening. It was barely ten feet from the road. Across the entrance was a broken chain link fence that Dean told us had been cut through years before by teenagers who liked to hang out in the cave to drink or have clandestine amorous encounters. We could see the glow of broken beer bottles and the white of paper trash just inside the entrance. We could smell rotting food. I hoped that was all we smelled.

Since the cave was man-made, we felt no ill effects. We walked in, carefully stepping over the broken bottles and trash. Garrett stayed outside.

As we moved further in from the entrance it was getting dark, and the floor was cleaner. Dean pulled a wand out of his coat pocket. It was only six or seven inches long and looked like a small tree branch, but when he held it up the tip glowed as bright as a streetlamp, illuminating the mine all around us.

"That's really cool," I told Dean.

"Thanks. This will make it easier to walk through here. The ground can be pretty uneven in these old mines."

We must have walked several hundred yards and we noticed some light coming down from above.

"That is an air shaft the miners put in to get air down here. It is also an emergency exit if there is a cave in. There is one more around a quarter mile in. We are around a hundred feet under the hill. These shafts are barred over up top so no one can fall in accidentally."

Bell asked. "How deep are these mines?"

"This one goes in almost a mile and slops down nearly a hundred feet further in. There are a couple of side tunnels too. If I do not feel any vibrations from Del and Dria in the next quarter mile, we'll go back and try the other mine."

I looked down. "It looks like there's been quite a few people walking through here. Look at all the footprints."

"Yes. There are quite a few who come into these mines still searching for gold. Probably like the old guys that hang out at the Saint George bar."

We walked further. I was still holding Granny's hand, keeping her from wearing out. This was a lot of walking for her. I was surprised that Dean could keep going, but being a wizard, he could probably go all day.

Finally, Dean stopped, waved his wand in a circle, then turned to us. "This is far enough. I cannot feel any presence anywhere in here. Oh," he looked at our hands. "And your rings are not glowing either. Let's go back and try the other mine."

When we exited, we were met by Garrett, who was sitting on a rock just outside the mine.

Granny seemed glad to see him. "Garrett. I thought you were going to join us."

"Sorry to say, I am a little claustrophobic. I would not have been much help in there."

"Dean, Bell, Charles, you go on. I'll head back down the hill with Garrett. It will be easier for you to go on without having to worry about me. You all please be careful."

"You'll be okay Granny?"

"Oh yes. Garrett doesn't have your Ohlone healing power, but he does have a strengthening spell that works about as well. Don't worry. It's all downhill. I'll see you when you get back to the hotel."

As she and Garrett headed down hill, hand in hand, the rest of us headed up the dirt road to the second mine. It was more than a half mile up a steep incline and even Bell and I were a little winded when we arrived. Dean wasn't even breathing hard.

This mine was sealed with old hand-made brick and a rusty metal door that was locked with a large, very old looking padlock.

"Looks pretty sealed up," I mentioned to Dean. "Need help to open it?"

"No. I got it. We can go in… right now."

Dean pulled out his small wand and tapped the lock. It opened and dropped to the ground. He tapped the door and it also opened with a loud creak that echoed back and forth in the mine and outside against the hillsides.

"Ah. I didn't want to do that." Dean frowned. "We'll have to hurry if one or more of those old miners heard that and show up. They still work this mine."

Dean again lifted his short wand and illuminated our way. This mine had a narrow rail line running through it, and less than twenty feet in we had to squeeze by a mine cart.

I noticed something. "This cart is half full. Look at that."

"Gold ore. There is gold ore mixed in the dirt. Like I said, those old guys are still working this mine. Come on. Let us keep going."

We were barely able to go a hundred feet when we were

stopped by a recent cave in. It appeared that someone had been digging through it and discovered the gold ore that came down with the cave in. The gold ore in the mine cart.

"Well. We cannot go any farther. That is disappointing. My wizard magic cannot move that much earth. Let us head back."

As soon as Dean said that we heard the loud echoing creak of the metal door being shut.

"What the hell!" I exclaimed.

"I was afraid when I opened the door someone would hear it."

Bell seemed unfazed. She closed her eyes. "There's two of them out there. They have rifles. Come. Let's go."

Dean looked at Bell with an odd look on his face. "Are you serious? You can see them? How about you, Charles? Can you see them too?"

"Nope. Bell has many abilities I don't have. She's amazing." Bell turned and gave me a quick kiss on the cheek.

We walked back toward the sealed entrance.

"They've gone," Bell said. "I'm sure they'll be back when they hear the door open. We'll have to be ready."

"The door is locked on the outside. I cannot use my wand through that steel door to unlock it."

"Bell can unlock it." I said.

"Really?"

"Piece of cake," I told Dean. "Watch."

Bell put her hand on the door and recited her unlocking incantation. We heard the lock open and drop again.

"Quickly. Push the door open and let's get ready to meet up with the two old miners," Bell instructed us.

We all pushed the door open. The loud creaking sound again

echoed through the hills. I heard someone yell down the road and heard footsteps quickly heading our way.

This time we were ready for them. When we saw them trotting up toward us with their rifles lifted like they were ready to fire, Dean waved his little wand and both rifles fell out of their hands and skittered into the bushes. The two old guys swore and tried to scramble over to grab them, but the bushes were thorny wild raspberries and put bloody scratches on their hands and they quickly pulled them back. We walked up to them, and I put a quick binding spell on them that made them think they just collapsed from exhaustion. They sat down on the dirt road and looked very dejected. They glanced up and noticed Dean.

"Dean! What the hell are you doing in our mine?"

"Sorry, boys, but we're looking for my nephew and his daughter who have disappeared. We were worried they might have… uh, fallen down one of the old air shafts."

"There're no air shafts in this mine. Those were filled up years ago. You didn't take anything out of there, did you?"

"Tom, Ernie, your gold is safe. We didn't touch it."

"Uh… what gold?"

I looked into their eyes and could see they wanted to keep this mine a secret.

Bell waved her hand. "We will be leaving. You can resume working in your mine when we are gone."

Both the old guys closed their eyes and laid down where they sat.

"Uh… Bell. What did you just do?" Dean asked. I was curious too.

"Hypnosis. They'll wake as soon as we're gone."

We were at least a hundred feet down the hill when we heard the squeak of the iron door open again. Old Tom and Ernie were heading into their mine to dig out some more gold.

Twenty minutes later we had made it back to the hotel. The three of us went into the main building and walked into the bar. There sat Granny and Garrett with mixed drinks in their hands talking and laughing. Only three of the old miners were left at the bar, still sipping shots from another nearly full whiskey bottle. We knew the other two were up the hill at their mine.

"Hi Granny. You look like you made it back okay. You don't look tired at all. Hi Garrett."

"I'm fine Charles dear. This Harvey Wallbanger is quite refreshing and rejuvenating." Granny got serious. "Dean. Did you have any luck?"

"No. The second mine had a cave in barely a hundred feet in. We had a run in with two of those old miners we've seen drinking whiskey here at the bar. They pointed guns at us, but I was able to disarm them with a little…" Dean whispered. "…magic."

Garrett asked, "Why were they pointing guns at you?"

Dean kept whispering. "Gold. That cave in brought down a vein of gold that those old guys are mining. There's enough gold there to keep them in whiskey for years… if they should live that long drinking so much."

Granny's turn to ask. "Where should we all look now?"

"I really don't know," Dean admitted. "I do keep getting short signals, almost like static, that Del and Dria are not far away."

I had an idea. "When Bell and I first got here and took a walk around town, we had a strange feeling walking a little way up Consolation Street. It was like a slight electrical charge. Wasn't it

Bell?"

"Yes. That's just what it felt like. And both our rings glowed."

Granny set her drink down. "Oh. Dear ones. You must be careful. If they glow too brightly, there's no telling what could happen. The old wive's tale… or rather old witch's tale… yes, this old witch's tale is that these rings might transfer you to a different place or time. Garret and I were talking about that very thing."

Dean's eyes went wide with excitement. "If, as you say Charles, you and Bell had an odd feeling on Consolation Street, show me where? Maybe that area has something to do with Del's and Dria's disappearance."

Chapter 8

Granny had seen our rings glow once before and told us it was nothing. Now she told us something different, and she and Garrett wanted to see if they would experience the same electrical charge Bell and I felt earlier. Dean just wanted to see if it had anything to do with his missing family members.

As soon as we were all together in front of the hotel, we started walking up Main. When we turned right on Consolation Street, we were met by the sight of three familiar new cars parked in front of the Volcano Union Pub and Inn. Two Mercedes sedans and a Porsche 911.

"Oh crap! It's the weird Wheelers and their minions!" I exclaimed. "What the hell are they doing here? Did they somehow follow us?"

We had told Granny about them, but Garrett wondered what

was so strange about them being in Volcano. Bell and I told them.

"Let me go in and check it out," Dean volunteered. "I know the owner and some of the staff in there. I will act like I am just stopping in to say hi and see if I can determine what they're up to."

"I will go with you," Garrett offered. "Maybe between your wizard and my warlock abilities, we can find out why they are here."

Bell, Granny, and I quietly moved to the side of the building where we were out of sight of the bar. We didn't want to take the chance of them recognizing us.

Fifteen minutes later Dean and Garrett came out and walked over to where we were waiting.

"They are all checked into the Inn here," Dean said. "You are right, Charles, those are very weird people. How many did you say were at Del's house?"

"Six. The two Wheelers, their son and his girlfriend, and the two Del had no idea who they are."

"Well, there are seven in there discussing something about a retreat," Garrett said.

"Volcano. Retreat," Bell said looking at me. "The sign on the Santa Cruz Elm Street Mission door."

"Could that Elm Street holy roller place be associated with the Wheelers?" I wondered.

"That must be the pastor from that church you mentioned that the Wheelers are talking to in there," Dean said. "He was wearing a dog collar. A clerical collar."

Garrett continued, "He seems to be a real pastor. However, he emits power of some kind. He is not a warlock, and Dean said he couldn't be a wizard. Whatever he is, he could not tell that Dean and I have abilities. I am not too sure about that other couple in there. They had dark glasses on so I could not take a look into their eyes. However, I felt they both kept staring at us."

Dean then suggested we go ahead and walk up the road. "Those people in there are too busy drinking to notice us. Let us continue with our plan to check out where your rings glowed."

We walked further up the road, which was fairly flat. Granny was able to keep up without getting winded. After crossing Plug Street, the pavement changed and was not in good shape. Several ankle-twisting potholes were along our route, and we had to be careful where we stepped.

"That's the place our rings glowed up ahead by that big oak tree." Bell pointed.

We stopped by the oak tree.

"I'm not feeling anything." Granny commented. "Garrett? Dean?"

"Nope."

"No. I am pretty sure I would not feel anything like you all can," Dean said.

Bell put her left arm around my shoulder, and we compared the rings on our right hands. Nothing. No glowing.

"Nothing," Bell and I both said at the same time.

"Sorry, Dean. I know we all hoped this would be a clue to finding Del and Dria," I said. "Let's head back."

Dean was looking around the area then took out his little wand and pointed it straight ahead of him as he turned in a full circle. The tip of his wand glowed when he pointed it northwest.

"Follow me. Well, maybe just you, Charles, and you Bell. Yana, it's a little bit of a climb up Church Street. Maybe you and Garrett should head back to the hotel."

"Nothing doing. We should all go," Granny insisted. "Charles can keep me going quite well as you saw when we went way up to those mines. If there's something up that street that's dangerous… well, it is possible… all our powers might be needed."

"Okay then. Let us go."

Church Street was a narrow rough-paved road heading up the hill.

"What's up here?" I asked Dean.

"Cemeteries. The first one is the Pioneer cemetery, and the upper one is the Catholic one. Both date back to the gold rush days. My wand pointed in this direction. Bell? Charles? Anything happening with your rings?"

"Nothing yet," I said.

"Yes, there is," Bell said.

I looked down at her hand and noticed a faint glow as she cupped her other hand around the ring shielding it from the sun. I moved my ring close to hers and shielded it. Yes, both rings were faintly glowing.

Granny, Garrett, and Dean gathered around to look. Granny suggested we head up to the Pioneer Cemetery and see if the rings got brighter.

Halfway there, our rings got brighter.

"Granny. Can you feel that? I'm getting a slight tingling sensation. You too Bell? Yeah. Garrett? Do you feel it?"

"I can't feel it. How about you Yana?"

"No. But look. Dean's wand is also glowing more. Dean, do

you feel any tingling?"

"No. I do not get that kind of feeling at all. It looks like the rings Charles and Bell have are causing their strange feelings. Maybe we should proceed more cautiously. Let us stop every few feet to see if their rings glow more or if that odd sensation gets worse for you all. If it gets too intense, we should retreat and figure out what to do next."

Bell and I looked at each other. I grabbed my medicine bag and her hand. "Let's go on."

After another ten steps we checked our rings. No change.

Once more Dean spun in a circle holding his wand out in front of him. This time the tip glowed in a different direction. Southeast.

"What the…!" Dean exclaimed. "Now my wand points back to where we started!" Clearly Dean was getting frustrated. Granny and Garrett noticed that too. They both went to Dean and put their hands on each of his shoulders. I held on to my medicine bag and reached out to take Dean's hand. In my mind I recited an Ohlone healing spell, and it took effect right away. Dean took a deep breath, looked at me, and said, "Thank you. Mister Blue. You and your lovely Bell are quite the pair. Let us all head back to the hotel. It is getting late, and I am sure you are all tired and hungry."

Chapter 9

Walking back to the hotel we once more passed the Volcano Union Pub and Inn. This time the three new cars were gone.

"Now where the hell have they gone?" I asked no one in particular. I thought it was odd they drove off already.

"They were pretty liquored up when Dean and I went in there," Garrett said. "I would not want to be on the same road they are driving on."

"I wonder if that Elm Street Mission pastor is still there," I mentioned to Dean.

"I will go in and check with Tammy at the front desk."

Dean went in before we could reply to him.

He was barely gone two minutes then returned shaking his head.

"No one from Santa Cruz has signed in. That group of people

wrote on the register that they are from Oakland. That guy with the collar is still in the bar. I asked Tammy if he was staying at the Inn. She said he was and noted by the signature he wrote Sutter Creek as his address."

"Charles." Bell grabbed my hand. "Let's go in and get a drink and I can try to read that guy's mind. I'll try to listen to his thoughts telepathically. We need to know if he is responsible for that bright flash and car fire in Santa Cruz. After all, it came from the direction of his church."

I agreed and told the others to wait for us in the Saint George Hotel bar. "Go ahead and order some food. We should meet up with you in twenty minutes or so."

"Be careful in there, dear ones," Granny said. "We still don't know who or what we're up against."

Bell and I went into the pub after the others had walked on down the street.

There was one other nondescript couple sitting at a table. The pastor, if that is what he was, was sitting alone at the bar. We sat at the bar with one bench between us and him. We ordered two glasses of Amador County Zinfandel and took a sip. Finally, some really good wine.

I glanced over as the pastor turned his head and looked at us. He smiled and nodded in a silent greeting. I took a quick look at his eyes and saw nothing.

Bell didn't have to look at him. She closed her eyes, and I telepathically heard her say an incantation to listen to his thoughts.

Barely a minute later, she opened her eyes and told me telepathically that the guy is interesting.

"*Interesting?*" I questioned, also telepathically.

"*Yeah. Let's finish our drinks and head back to the hotel. I'll reveal what I heard to you when we meet up with the others.*"

Both of us took our time finishing our wine. We were both surprised how good the Amador Zin was. I asked the bartender where the winery was, and he said it was in an old gold rush town called Plymouth. The vineyard had been planted by Italian immigrants in the 1860s. And here I thought the best California wines were only in the Napa and Sonoma regions.

After draining our glasses, we left a tip, and headed back to the hotel bar where the others were waiting for us. Everyone was hungry, so we ordered food.

As we waited for our food to arrive, Bell leaned forward on the table and told the group what she found out.

"First item. The guy's name is Reverend Paul Stagnaro. And, no, Charles, he is not related to the fishing and restaurant Stagnaros in Santa Cruz. His Elm Street Mission is a sanctuary for the down and out and homeless. He and his volunteers serve a single meal every afternoon for them as he sometimes reads the Bible to them. He also tries to find work for those who are able. He has another church in Sutter Creek. That's why he signed the register with that address."

"Sounds like he's both religious and civic minded," I said. "Also, I did get the feeling he does have some kind of ability."

"That I couldn't tell from his thoughts. What I did get is the second item. We wondered why he was talking to the Wheelers and the others. They forced themselves on him trying to convince him to let them use his Santa Cruz mission for their meetings. They also said they were in Volcano to... get this... find Del.

Dean, somehow, they found out Del came here. They may have driven up to your place looking for him."

I had a suggestion. "Dean. Let me drive you home. If the Wheelers are there, no telling what that drunken dysfunctional group could do. I wouldn't put it past them to break in… or even lay in wait for you to return thinking Del is with you. You might need help."

"I'll go too," Bell said.

"I want to go," Granny said.

"Me too," said Garrett.

"Thank you everyone. It is really not necessary. If they are at my place, I can take care of them quite easily." Dean pulled his little wand out then quickly slipped it back in his pocket as our waitress arrived and started serving our food.

Granny and Garrett both got mac and cheese. Dean got a BLTA, a BLT with avocado. Bell and I both got cheeseburgers. Thick, medium-rare, hand-made patties with cheddar and all the fixings, tomato, pickle, grilled onions, and lettuce with a thousand island type of sauce, on a square sourdough roll. The cheeseburgers were really good. Even the fries were excellent. Bell and I ooed and awed with each bite. Granny and Garrett laughed at our culinary pleasures. Dean smiled then copied our ooing while biting into his BLTA.

I finished my food and pushed my plate away. As I lifted my wine glass to my lips, I noticed a white cat at the open front door staring at me.

"Bell. Look over there at the door. It's Freesia."

The others turned to look.

"Such a beautiful cat," Garrett said.

"Thank you, Mister Stone," Freesia said telepathically.

"Wha...?" Garrett's eyes went wide.

"Hello Freesia," Bell said. *"Is Madam Seren here?"*

"Yes, Mistress Beltane. She checked in and is next to your rooms. She is in the Emigrant Room." Freesia looked at Granny. *"Madam Seren would like to speak to you, Madam Blue, as soon as you are finished eating."*

"Dear Freesia. Thank you. Please tell Gwyn... Madam Seren, I will be there shortly."

"Yes. I just told her."

With that, Freesia left.

Garrett stared at me and Bell with a questioning look. *"Talking cat?"*

"A human turned into a cat," Bell told Garrett telepathically.

"What is going on?" Dean asked. "Why were you all staring at that cat?"

Bell answered in a whisper. "Ah. I guess you wizards cannot converse telepathically. That white cat was once a young witch who was turned into that beautiful feline by an evil black witch. Pete Ramahi's mother. We are hoping we can break the spell and bring her back to her true self."

Chapter 10

Dean left shaking his head in disbelief. Because he wasn't able to speak or listen telepathically, it was hard for him to believe Freesia spoke to us. He told us before he left that even though wizards could perform many types of magic, they couldn't change anyone into an animal. I asked Dean to call if the Wheelers and their cohorts were at his place and if he needed help. He insisted he could take care of them.

I hoped he was right.

Granny, Garrett, Bell, and I finished our drinks and went back to our rooms. Garrett had secured a room called Poker Flat on the third floor in the main building.

After Bell and I brushed our teeth and did our other bathroom duties, we went outside to relax for a little while in the white painted Adirondack chairs on the front porch. Before we could sit down, Granny came out of her room, and Gwyn and Freesia came out of theirs.

"Yana, dear. It is so good to see you again. You look as young as you were in the Mystic Eye in San Francisco." Gwyn and Granny gave each other hugs. "And hello. Bell. Charles. Good to see you again too."

"Dear Gwyn. Are you picking up any visions here? Is that why you came to Volcano?"

"Yes, Yana, to both your questions. My strongest vision was of those drunken sots, the Wheelers, who left Santa Cruz and came here with those two other couples. I saw that they are here to find Del, whom I know is missing. Sort of."

"Sort of?" I asked as we made our way to one of the picnic tables in the yard between the two Saint George Hotel buildings.

"Yes. I am getting feelings that he and his daughter, Dria, are close. But do not worry. I feel that the Wheelers and their underlings will not be able to find them!" Gwyn said that last sentence with anger.

"Gwyn, have you run up against the Wheelers before?" Granny asked.

"Yes. Twice. Shortly after I moved to San José, twenty some years ago, they tried to extort money from me saying they would leave me alone to practice my psychic business I had there at that time. If I did not pay, they would send their followers to destroy my store. I refused to pay, but no one came after that. I saw in my crystal that nearly all of the Wheelers' followers were killed by the Ramahi family barely a week later. Just the other day, they tried to get to my boat, probably to try to extort money again. Freesia saw them and made sure they did not try to force their way onto the dock. She slipped under the gate and attacked them when they tried to pick her up. They both have some nice deep scratches on their arms and hands."

"Is Freesia okay?" Bell asked. "They didn't hurt her, did they?"

Freesia answered. *"Mistress Beltane, I am fine. They dropped me, but as a cat, I landed on my feet and hurried back under the gate and back to Madam Seren's boat. They were screaming and swearing at me but could not reach me. Hah."*

I'd swear that Freesia smiled. I had to ask Gwyn, "How did the Wheelers know where you live?"

"You were followed when you first came to visit. The Wheelers have had someone watching you all the way from San Francisco and in Santa Cruz."

"Really? Are you sure? Crud. Bell and I would have felt that someone was following us that whole time."

"I am afraid this person has abilities to shield herself from your sensing."

"Herself?" I asked.

"A witch?" Bell asked.

"That I cannot tell. She shields that part of herself from me too. Now. I would really like to talk to Yana. We have a lot to catch up on."

Bell and I got up from the picnic table and excused ourselves just as Garrett arrived. Granny introduced him to Gwyn, then he came over to Bell and me. I asked him, "Do you want to come with Bell and me to Dean's house? We're worried the Wheelers were there waiting for him and we want to make sure he's okay."

"Sure. I think between the three of us, if the Wheelers and their followers are there and have overpowered Dean, which I doubt, we could take care of them."

"Well, Dean said he didn't need help," I commented. "However, I have no idea how powerful his wizard magic is or how he uses it. We've never come across anyone like him before. He has that stick, his little wand, but what if it was taken from him? Would he be powerless? We need to see if he's okay."

The three of us headed for Dean's house.

"Look there. Two of those cars are back at the Inn. Hmm. The only one missing is the black Mercedes. I got a bad feeling. Uh… Bell, look at our rings."

Both rings were glowing.

Bell asked, "I don't feel anything. I mean there's no strange electric-like vibration. You?"

I answered, "No. Nothing. Now look. They stopped glowing."

Garrett was watching us with interest. "When we have time, I would really like to find out more about those rings."

For the next quarter mile up the hill, we kept quiet, watching around us in case someone was still following me and Bell.

We were almost to Dean's place when we saw the black Mercedes parked next to Dean's dragon mailbox. The motor was still running, but we didn't see anyone in the car. Dean's front door was open.

Bell mentioned to me and Garrett telepathically, *"I can't feel life forces. Something is wrong. We had better rush in quickly. Be prepared in case it's a trap."*

We all recited our own protection spells and ran up the stairs to the porch, through the open door, and rushed into the living area.

Dean lay unconscious, face down on his kitchen floor. A small pool of blood was under his head. Jerry and Terry Wheeler lay next to him, their bodies flattened and looking like old leather. They were completely drained of everything: bone, blood, organs. What was left looked like ancient dried-up mummies.

As we three stared at the disturbing sight, we heard the Mercedes peel out, make a sliding u-turn, and speed down the hill.

Bell and I ran out too late to see who took off in the car. Bell closed her eyes and mumbled an incantation. "Nothing. Whoever it is who did this is awfully powerful. I can't sense anything but rage. Charles, let's go in and make sure Dean is okay."

Garrett had already taken care of Dean. He was awake and sitting in a chair at his dining room table. His head was resting on his folded arms. He was also holding his wand. It was broken. He sadly looked up at us. His nose was broken, and drying blood from it covered half his face. He also had black eyes.

"Dean," I said. "Let me take you to urgent care in Sutter Creek. I can run downhill and get our van…"

"No. No. That is not necessary. I can heal myself quite easily. Charles, please pull my suitcase out from under my bed."

"Suitcase?"

"Please hurry!"

I went into Dean's small bedroom and slid an old brown Samsonite suitcase from under his narrow twin bed. I brought it in, and he motioned for me to put it on the table in front of him. He opened it up. It looked empty.

Dean waved his right hand over the case then reached in and pulled out another wand. This one also looked like a thin tree branch but was twice as long as his broken wand.

He tapped the wand against his nose. The swelling disappeared as did the black eyes. Dean sighed. "That really hurt."

Garrett put his hand on Dean's shoulder. "Did you see who attacked you and did that?" He pointed to the Wheelers.

"They did. When I came back home, they were in here hiding behind the door and clubbed me on the head with something, maybe my fireplace poker. I fell down stunned and they kicked me in the face. I started to raise my wand to protect myself, and one of them grabbed the end and broke it before I could concentrate. I felt something explode and I blacked out."

"You're okay now?" I asked. "You seem okay. You're in better shape than those two." I pointed at the Wheelers. "By the way. With their car out front, didn't you think they would be in your house?"

"There was no car out front when I got here. I did not expect them to be lying in wait for me. I am embarrassed. I was careless."

"The car was here when we arrived," Bell said. "The black Mercedes. It tore off when we came in and found you. Should we call the police?"

Dean shook his head. "No. There are no police here in town. We have a sheriff who patrols around the area, but he is close to retirement. He only knows how to write tickets for traffic violations. He would not understand what happened here. Neither would the sheriffs in the main office in Sutter Creek. Whatever happened to the Wheelers was done magically… by either a wizard I do not know about, or some avenging demon. It is up to us to solve this mystery… after we find Del and Dria."

Chapter 11

While we were all staring at the Wheelers' bodies and wondering what to do with them, Bell and I felt a sudden disturbance. Our rings were glowing quite brightly, and we felt what seemed like an electrical charge. Garrett shivered. He was feeling it too.

As suddenly as it started, it stopped.

"What the hell was that?" Garrett asked. "I felt like I was getting shocked. Dean, did you feel that?"

"A little. I did feel something like static. Also, my wand did glow like your rings for a few seconds."

"This has been happening to Bell and me several times now. Each time it's been at a different location around Volcano. There's got to be a reason for it."

"For now," interjected Garrett. "What about those bodies? Should we bury them?"

"I'll take care of it," Dean said. He waved his wand. The bodies disappeared.

"What?" Garrett, wide eyed, exclaimed.

"Wow!" Bell was also wide eyed.

"Jeezus!" I nearly yelled. "Granny couldn't even do that."

"I couldn't?"

"Granny! How did you get up here? Are you okay? You don't seem winded."

"We didn't walk. Gwyn drove us here in her little VW bug. You didn't hear us drive up?"

Gwyn walked in. "I had a vision of something happening here. Being only a short distance away, it was a strong vision. Yana and I knew we had to come up here. So. Where are the bodies?"

"I sent them on their way," Dean told Gwyn. " Where no one will ever find them."

"And where can that be?" Granny asked.

"I should not say. Well... Oh hell. Since I am probably the last wizard alive here..." Dean sighed. "There is another time and place where wizards originally came from. It is where we were once born and trained eons ago. Since no other wizards exist there anymore, I sent the Wheelers there."

"Really?" I questioned. "Dean, I probably shouldn't ask, but what happened to the other wizards?"

Dean looked down. A heavy sadness came over him. "A... a plague. A plague that destroyed our entire magical community. It was started by an evil power-hungry sorceress. She tried to weaken us so we would be under her control. It backfired on her. Everyone lost their powers and could not protect themselves from sickness. I only escaped because I was here and not there at the time."

"What happened to the sorceress?" I asked.

"I do not know. Maybe the plague took her too. I try to be pacifistic, but because of all the pain and suffering she caused, I hope she died a horrible death!" Dean's sadness had turned to anger. He glanced at the rest of us and took a deep breath to center himself. "Sorry for the outburst. That is not like me."

Granny came up to Dean and hugged him. "Dean, is it possible Del and his children could have wizarding powers?" she asked. "After all, you are related to them."

Dean sighed. "That I do not know. Del and his children were only taught a little of your type of power from Del's father. If they had been brought up in the wizarding time, or were sent there when younger, maybe they could have been decent wizards. I really do not know. I… I have to find them."

I had been listening to Dean but was thinking of something else. I came over and whispered in Granny's ear. "Uh… Granny. Did you feel anything strange come over you when you and Gwyn were driving here?"

"Why, yes, I did. Just before we arrived, I felt a slight shock. I thought it was just static from Gwyn's car. Why?"

"Our rings glowed very brightly, brighter than those other times we've experienced here, and Bell and I felt a stronger shock. Garrett felt it too. Dean says he even felt it a little. His wand glowed for a few seconds. And now, someone attacked and killed the Wheelers. I wish we could figure out what is going on. What the hell have we gotten ourselves into this time?"

No one could answer.

Granny hopped in Gwyn's VW, and they headed back to the hotel. I asked Dean if he wanted to walk back with us, but he said he wanted to stay to clean up the mess left behind by the Wheelers when they ransacked his house. He had also noticed some items on his bookshelf had been moved and a few pieces were broken like maybe the Wheelers had been looking for something.

Bell, Garrett, and I said our goodbyes and then asked Dean to come to the hotel for breakfast in the morning with us. He said he would think about it.

On our walk back, I voiced a concern. "Say. Don't you think the Wheelers' son will wonder where they disappeared to?"

"That may be a problem," Garrett admitted.

"No problem at all." Bell surprised me and Garrett when she said that. "Charles. You know what to do. Your grandfather, Peter Red Feather's spirit, can guide you."

"Of course. I was only thinking as a warlock and not as a shaman. As much as I don't want to confront that Wheeler kid and the others, we don't want them alerting the authorities about missing persons. Yeah. It will be medicine bag time."

When we reached the end of Emigrant Road, we looked over at the Volcano Union Pub and Inn and saw the Porsche and the white Mercedes parked in front.

"Let's go in the bar and see if they know about the Wheelers missing or not," I suggested. "Garrett, why don't you head back to the hotel and let Granny know where we are."

"I would like to go in there with you. If there is a problem, I can help. I can be formidable if need be."

The three of us walked into the bar only to find one other

person there. Reverend Paul Stagnaro. He looked at us and smiled. "Hello Miss Beltane, Mister Blue, Mister Stone. Please join me."

"How did you know our names?" Garrett asked.

"Miss Beltane. When you came in to… how should I put this… check me out, I let you see what I allowed you to see. Now. Mister Blue. You look into my eyes. Tell me what you see."

The Reverend looked straight at me.

"I see nothing. You're blocking me. Who are you?"

"I really am Reverend Paul Stagnaro. And I do own and run the Elm Street Mission in Santa Cruz as well as the Generation Life Mission in Sutter Creek. I am also a Miwoc shaman as were my father, grandfather, and other relations before me. Mister Blue, like yours, my medicine bag holds their spirits. At my churches, I heal and protect the homeless, the depressed, and the down and out. Now. You want to know about that destructive flash of white light that you think came from my Elm Street Mission."

"That is why we're in Volcano," I said.

"First, get yourself something to drink. The Amador zin and pinot are excellent. Second, I must tell you, that light did not come from my church. My guiding spirit told me it came from a black sports car parked in front of it."

"Uh… guiding spirit?" Garrett asked the question before I could tell him about my guiding spirit, my grandfather Peter Red Feather. The Reverend turned to me to explain.

"Mister Blue, I am sure your Ohlone heritage allows you to conjure up your guiding spirit to watch over you, your family and your home like my Miwok heritage does. Unfortunately, witches and warlocks do not have guiding spirits. Charles, you are an exception because of your grandparents. One Indian and one witch. Anyway, normally witches and warlocks can only conjure up spirits, sometimes demonic. No, not you Miss Blue, Yana, and you Miss Beltane. You are both good witches."

"Reverend Stagnaro. Please call me Bell."

"Okay, Bell. And call me Paul. As I was about to say, it is the black art practitioners who do nearly all the demonic conjuring. I would say that whoever, or whatever caused the flash and explosion might have been a conjured evil spirit, maybe working as an assassin. Used once then removed… or disappeared, leaving no trace."

"We think that whatever destroyed the van did not destroy young Marty," Bell said. "No cremated body was found in the bus's ashes. We are hopeful Marty was transported somewhere. Unfortunately, his father and sister are now missing too."

The Reverend pulled his medicine bag out from under his shirt and held on to it. He closed his eyes and spoke in the Miwok language. It was so different from the Ohlone I spoke, so I couldn't understand the words. I did get a feeling of what he was doing though.

"I am told the answer can be found in the Masonic caves."

Chapter 12

Caves. Natural caves. Not the kind of place a warlock or witch want to be, according to Granny. I know she prepared us for such a journey, but I didn't like the idea of the possibility of losing power, even with Granny's so-called protection. Can it really happen?

After Reverend Stagnaro, Paul, told us about checking the Masonic caves, he excused himself and headed upstairs to his room. He said he needed rest after consulting with his spirit. Whether this was true or not, I didn't know. I never needed rest after I consulted with my grandfather.

As soon as he left, the Wheeler's son, Nicolas, his girlfriend, and the other couple came into the bar and ordered mixed drinks all around. Bell and I moved to a booth so they couldn't see us, but we could still hear their loud inebriated voices. Since none of them had seen Garrett, he sat on the other side and was able to watch them. The young man looked worried and kept looking at the door and conferring with his girlfriend, who we found out from listening, was named Rhea. He was obviously concerned about his parents not returning. We heard the other couple tell him not to worry, because the Wheelers are probably drumming up more business for them.

I spoke to Bell and Garrett telepathically. *"You hear that? Drumming up business? Garrett, can you see anything about those two. No? Bell, remember when we went to Del's house and those people were there? We both felt something was odd about them. I wonder if they have abilities of some kind."*

Bell told Garrett and me, *"We should sneak out of here and head back to the hotel before we're noticed."*

"Let me do one thing first." I glanced at Nicolas Wheeler and held my medicine bag. I telepathically recited an Ohlone spell to ease his mind. I was afraid I was too far away, but it did seem to work. He sighed, smiled, and started talking to his girlfriend more. As we headed out, I noticed the odd couple had turned around and looked like they were following me through their dark glasses. I had a terrible feeling they sensed what I did.

When we entered the St. George Hotel, I could hear Granny and Gwyn talking and laughing. I also heard several other voices gabbing away in the saloon. The five old miners at the bar turned to see us and stopped talking. I'd swear they were all giving us the evil eye. They quickly downed their drinks, then got up and left.

I noticed as they left that two of them were carrying. They had cowboy looking belts and holsters with revolvers in them. They were both resting their right hands on the gun handles like they were ready for a gun fight. I watched two of them get into an old faded red International Harvester pickup. The cracked back window had a gun rack with two rifles. The three other guys got into a rusty looking old GMC pickup. It also had a gun rack in the back window with one rifle and a fishing pole. Both pickups belched a lot of white smoke from their exhausts as they pulled away.

And in the white smoke I thought I saw a figure. If I did see something, it wasn't there anymore once the exhaust smoke dissipated. Bell tapped me on the shoulder.

"Look at our rings." They were glowing then quickly faded. "I didn't feel any kind of static that time. Did you?"

"No. I didn't feel anything either. I was watching those guys take off in those old pickups and thought I saw something ghostly in the smoke they belched. Garrett, did you feel anything?"

"Not a thing."

Granny and Gwyn were looking at me. Gwyn spoke. "Charles. Yana and I also saw that phantom figure in the smoke. I heard it speak to us in my head too. It is Del."

"Del?" Bell and I both questioned. I continued questioning. "So, is Del dead? Does his spirit have unfinished business here on earth?"

"No, dear Charles," Granny answered. "Gwyn was just telling me about another dimension, the phantom dimension she called it, where she gets some of her psychic references. Some seance practitioners say it's the dead speaking, but that's not really possible."

We hadn't noticed that Dean had come in and joined us and stood behind me and Bell. I would swear he just appeared out of nowhere.

Dean interjected, "No, Yana, Gwyn, that is not a phantom dimension. That is the wizard world. It is in another time and is identical to our own. Gwyn, if Del is there, as you say, there is a reason. His daughter Dria should be there too. Maybe his son Marty is too."

"Isn't that where you sent the Wheelers' bodies?" I asked.

"I did. I did not feel that anyone was there. I will have to go back there and make sure they did not scare Del and Dria. It has been nearly a century since I have been there. Since the sorceress plague destroyed all the wizards, I had no reason to return. Even now, it will be hard to adjust to that realm. But I must go and bring back Del and Dria, and, hopefully, Marty too… if that is where they are."

Out of curiosity, I had to ask, "How do you go there? Do you just wave your wand and vanish?"

Dean smiled, but it quickly faded. "Well, sort of. I was able to send the Wheelers there easily because their bodies were just empty shells. For me to go there, I used to transport myself in the old days, but because it has been so long, it is better to use a portal. There are a few of them around the world. Usually in caves. The one here is in the largest and topmost of the Masonic caves. And, yes, I wave my wand, but I don't vanish. My wand opens the portal I can walk through. The old gold rush Masons in this town knew that certain caves were special. That's why they started to have meetings there. However, after four or five meetings, even the Masons got spooked by their candles and lanterns suddenly extinguishing. They moved back into town and were able to share a new building with the Odd Fellows for several years until the gold ran out and everyone left. So... any of you want to accompany me to the wizard world?"

Granny, Gwyn, and Garrett all shook their heads no. Bell and I looked at each other and we both raised our hands.

"Ah. You two want to go?"

"Yeah, but we'll need to prepare ourselves with Granny's cave protection goodies. We don't want to lose our powers."

"Uh, I hate to say this, but I have been... well, lying to you. I will tell you more about that later. Now, you don't need to worry about your protection items."

"Really?" I questioned. "So that cave-is-dangerous stuff is not real?"

Dean shrugged and looked down at his feet. "I am sorry I had to start that rumor. I wanted to make sure no one... well, others like yourselves, from accidently discovering any of the portals. I am so sorry to have been so cautious around you."

"Dean." Bell put her hand on his shoulder. "No worries. We understand. Right Charles?" Bell looked at me. I reluctantly nodded yes. "When do you want to start?"

"It is too late to go there now. We should start right after breakfast tomorrow."

Granny warned us to be careful and should probably use the stuff she brought for cave protection anyway. When I turned back to talk to Dean about it, he was gone... as quickly and as silently as he arrived.

It was late and we were all thinking of turning in. We got up, but before we could go to our rooms, we heard a commotion outside. We all went out the door to the wood sidewalk in front of the hotel.

The young woman who worked the front desk at the Volcano Union Pub and Inn, who I think Dean said was Tammy, was running toward us up the street crying and yelling something about someone dying. Her face was white with fright. The bartender from the same pub was running behind her trying to get her to stop. Other people from the country store and the bakery were standing outside and watching and wondering what was going on.

As they headed toward us, I grabbed my medicine bag and quickly recited an Ohlone soothing spell. The girl and bartender slowed and stopped in front of us. They both sighed.

I asked them very calmly and quietly, "What has happened?"

The bartender answered as if in a trance, which he was. "A body. Sitting at a picnic table behind the Inn. He looked f... flat..."

The trance wore off too quickly. Panic returned to the girl. She started to run off again, and Bell jumped in and recited a quick spell. This put them both into a hypnotic sleep. I gave one more spell to relax them from their terrible finding. Bell and I made sure we got them sitting down on one of the benches in front of the hotel.

Bell and I ran down the street to the Union Pub and Inn followed by Granny, Gwyn and Garrett at a much slower pace.

We went around to the back of the pub and there, two people were sitting on one side of the picnic table. It was the Wheelers' son Nicolas and his girlfriend, Rhea, who seemed in shock. Nicolas was bending over and leaning face down and was flattened like his parents were. No bone. No blood. Nothing but mummified skin. *Why did Tegan kill the young Wheeler?*

Too many people witnessed this. There was no way we could hide this from the Amador County sheriff this time.

Chapter 13

Someone had already called 911. I could hear a siren in the distance echoing through the hills. In the darkness I could just make out its flashing lights coming up the hill toward town. Within five minutes, a four-wheel drive olive-green Jeep Cherokee with a sheriff department insignia on the side pulled up in front of the Volcano Union Pub and Inn. An elderly, thin man, who looked too old and frail to still be a sheriff, got out and walked through the Inn to the back picnic area where we were standing. The name plate on his jacket said Jackson.

"Awright," Sheriff Jackson said. "What the hell is goin' on here… Holy shit!"

As soon as Sheriff Jackson saw the body, his face turned white and he quickly turned away, ran around the corner of the building and we heard him upchucking. He went to his Jeep and we heard him loudly call for backup. I feared some real Amador sheriffs would be arriving from Sutter Creek soon.

I looked at Bell, Granny, Gwyn, and Garrett, hoping between us we could cover it up somehow. Dean was back, again appearing out of nowhere and startling us. As I took a deep breath to calm my surprise, I asked, "Is there anything we can do here before the sheriffs arrive? And what about the girl?"

Dean suggested, "Look. I've met a couple of the sheriffs in this county. Why don't you all go back to the hotel and let me take care of this. I might have to do some wizard stuff to keep this quiet."

I also had a suggestion. "Bell and I should stay with you. Bell's powers could be a great help, and my medicine bag could help too. Especially for his girlfriend. We could make the sheriffs see only what we want them to see."

"We're not leaving either," Granny said. "Gwyn can keep a lookout, maybe through Freesia. Garrett and I can combine our powers with Bell's and Charles's and quadruple our chances of quieting this down."

We'd never combined our powers before, and I hoped Granny knew how. Gwyn sensed my concern. "Do not worry, Charles. Yana knows what to do. It is old school to her. I sense Bell already knows what to do too. She will guide you."

Granny nodded. "Ah, yes. You're correct Gwyn. Bell's mother, Constance, taught her well. Anyway, dear Charles, this combining of powers used to be quite common in the old days when we were fighting for our lives."

"Fighting for your lives? With who? Where?"

"Charles, my dear grandson. I've never told you this because it was so long ago when Constance, Garrett, and I were young friends. We never talked about it because it is hard to relive those dark times. With what is happening with Del and his children and these Wheeler deaths, it may be happening again. I think it's time for you to know our story. When we were in our twenties, a large faction of fundamentalists, kind of like those here in these shells of bodies, hired assassins to wipe us out. These weren't just any human assassins, they were witches and warlocks who were, we think, trained by a banned sorceress. Yes, Dean, she was the same who caused the plague that killed all your kind. We survived only because we worked to combine all our powers to combat them. It was successful enough that the remaining assassins left us alone… or disappeared. However, those two that were with the Wheelers might be a return of the same kind of assassins."

"Holy sh… cow, Granny! Really? They didn't seem that dangerous to us. They also drank as much as the Wheelers. Say, if the Wheelers hired them, why were they targeted? Did their assassins turn on them?"

"I was wondering that too," Garrett said. "Gwyn. Can you pick up any vibrations from… uh… Gwyn. Are you okay?"

Gwyn had sat down on a seat at a picnic table next to Nicolas Wheeler's body. She was leaning over with her head resting in her hands. Freesia was in her lap and her paw with gently stroking Gwyn's arm.

"Oh. Sorry Garrett. Freesia was telling me what she saw."

Bell and I looked at each other. "We've heard Freesia talk telepathically to us before. We didn't hear her this time."

"You have only heard her when she directed her thoughts

directly to you. She was only speaking to me this time. Anyway, Freesia saw what killed this boy. *Freesia, go ahead and tell them."*

"*As a cat, I like to be outside. I took a walk around the neighborhood, and just behind this Inn I noticed a couple sitting at a picnic table and talking. That couple there. They seemed to be arguing. I couldn't quite hear, so I started to come closer when a tall, pale woman who seemed to just appear behind those two. I backed into a bush to hide and watch. She reached out with both hands, putting them on his head. They tried to get up but couldn't. Suddenly the woman glowed for a split second then disappeared, leaving what remains of the man."*

"A tall pale woman," I said. "Why does that sound familiar?"

"You remember, don't you?" Bell tapped me on the head.

"Of course! The story Del told us about some woman who came to the gigs when Del was playing in the band with Pete Ramahi. Looked Goth. Hmm. *Say, Freesia. Did this pale woman have on dark lipstick and a black motorcycle jacket by any chance?"*

"*Why yes, Mister Blue. You know her?"*

"We heard a story about her from Del Prentiss, Dean's missing nephew. He told us she only came out at night."

"Bell, Del said it seemed Pete Ramahi had a thing for this pale woman. I wonder if she's a Ramahi follower?"

"If she is, she would have come after you first. She went after the Wheelers instead. Oh. Listen."

Sirens.

"Okay." Dean said while looking at Rhea then back to me. "Well… uh, let us get this show on the road. Uh… okay. Charles. Use your medicine bag to sooth… R… uh, that poor girl's shock."

Why was Dean stuttering?

Chapter 14

Two sheriff patrol cars and an ambulance pulled up in front of the Volcano Union Pub and Inn. The bartender had come back and had been talking to sheriff Jackson who told the other sheriffs that the bodies were in the back and to be prepared for what they'll see. They sped around the sharp turn up Emigrant Road and pulled up behind us.

There was only one sheriff in each car. Two medical techs got out of their ambulance and followed them to the crime scene.

Both sheriffs asked at the same time, "You haven't touched anything here, have you?"

Garrett answered. "No sirs. We were just making sure no wild animals or feral dogs got at them."

Nice lie, I thought.

They finally introduced themselves to us. "I'm Sheriff

Stoneman, and this is Sheriff Bridgeman. And you are?"

We took turns introducing ourselves, as Bridgeman took notes. He knew Dean.

"And... that is the body? Why was Sheriff Jackson so upset about it?"

Between the five of us, two witches, two warlocks, and a wizard, and before the sheriffs arrived, we were able to re-inflate the body to look like a normal corpse. I tried to soothe the girlfriend with one of my Ohlone spells, but she kept her head buried in her arms. Bell finally took the girl up to her room upstairs and put her to bed to sleep. Bell quickly came back and looked over at me with concern. Gwyn stood aside just inside the Inn's back door to keep a mental watch on the sheriffs and medical techs through Freesia.

Sheriff Stoneman asked, "Now. Who discovered the body? Any of you?"

"No." Bell answered. "It was the young woman who works here as a receptionist at the Inn's front desk. She heard a scream from this guy's girlfriend and came out here. Tammy, the receptionist was frightened by it and ran by us. The bartender didn't look that panicked, but I think he was trying to get to her to calm her down. I understand she is his daughter." Dean told us that.

Granny continued. "We came to see what the ruckus was about and discovered this guy. I think the bartender must have called it in, and that other sheriff arrived."

Sheriff Stoneman turned to Bridgeman. "Old Jackson sounded unnerved when he called it in. After being on light traffic duty all the time, he must not be used to seeing bodies."

He turned back to us. "So, where is this guy's girlfriend? We need to talk to her."

Bell answered, "I took her up to her room. She was… uh, freaking out. I think she is dozing." Bell couldn't say she attempted to put her to sleep by her hypnosis spell.

Bridgeman said, "We'll talk to her later then. Now, do any of you know this man?"

I answered this question. "We've seen him around, but don't know his name." I lied.

Stoneman pulled a pair of latex gloves out of his pocket and reached into Nicolas Wheeler's back pocket and gently slipped out a wallet.

"Let's see. No driver's license. Hmm. There is a medical card with an address. Look at this, Bridgeman." Sheriff Stoneman turned to us. "Uh… you all can leave after you let us know where you're staying in case we need to talk to you again."

As we were leaving, Gwyn put a finger to her head, and we noticed Freesia passing us and sat herself out of sight under the picnic table. *"She will keep us informed. Let's just go in here and find a table so we'll be close enough to hear Freesia's telepathic report."*

The bar was closed, but quite a few of the Inn's guests were hanging around to watch the activities. All of the tables were taken. Granny quietly said something in Romani and an elderly couple yawned, got up, and headed up stairs to their room. We all sat down at their vacated table.

"Ah. She's started."

"Madam Seren. My friends. The name of the young man is Nicolas Wheeler. He lived at 1226 Larchmont Lane in Daly City. He is showing the wallet to the other sheriff, and he whistled. Money. He is counting

it. Ten one-hundred-dollar bills. One thousand dollars. He put the wallet back. It appears he kept the money. Now the ambulance people were asked to come over and told to take the body away. Ah. They are told to take it to a police morgue in Sutter Creek for an autopsy."

"Autopsy," I whispered to the others. "What will happen when the coroner cuts into him?"

Granny answered. "Not to worry, dear Charles. They won't. After we made him look like a normal dead person, I also put a spell on him so no one can see that there is nothing inside his body. Dean's magic made sure he will be cremated tomorrow without the autopsy."

"That's a relief." I said with a sigh. I then noticed the time on the clock behind the bar. "Jeez. It's after midnight. Let's go back to our hotel and try to get some rest." Before we rose from the table I noticed Freesia sitting by herself outside the open back door, her eyes almost closed. She wasn't saying anything, and I had the feeling she was more tired than I was. I had to say something.

"What about her?" I pointed to Freesia. "We need to start thinking about helping her become human again."

"Thank you, Mister Blue." Freesia heard me, opened her eyes and looked up. *"I do want to be human again, but we must wait. I am in a good position to help when I can. As a cat, I can go places you cannot. Now, also as a cat, I must sleep much more than my human-like self did."* With that, she quietly padded away.

I looked at Bell and noticed tears in her eyes.

"Bell? What is wrong?"

"I just feel for Freesia. Her curse was caused by the same Ramahi family that came after your parents and put me in my death sleep for twenty years. She has been a cat now for over twenty years. I ache for her. No, Charles. Let go of your medicine bag. I'm okay. Let's go back to our room."

As soon as we went into our room and closed the door, Bell came up to me and gave me a big hug and planted a long, lingering kiss on me that caused me to feel my pants getting tight. It had been a while, but making love came back to me like riding a bike. I didn't even have to pedal hard, I just coasted. We finally dropped off to sleep after two in the morning.

We weren't able to sleep long. We were awakened by a knocking at the door. I looked at the radio clock by the bed. It was 3:30am.

"Who can be knocking at this hour?" I sleepily asked Bell.

I got up, slipped my pants and a t-shirt on and opened the door. I quickly stepped back, my eyes wide and my heart pounding.

It was the tall pale woman.

Chapter 15

Bell quickly got up and slipped into her jeans and sweatshirt and came to stand beside me.

The pale woman walked into our room but did not come toward us. She went over to the chair in the corner and sat down hard as if she were very tired. She had a sad look on her white face. She also looked older and not as Goth as I imagined from the descriptions.

"I'm so sorry to have startled you. I have been watching you, your family, and friends since you've been here. I think you have occasionally noticed my presence. Look at your rings."

Both our rings were glowing.

"I can see you are concerned. Please don't be. I am not a threat to you."

"Who are you?" Bell asked. "And why have you been noticed only at night?"

She sighed. "Over the years I've been called a wraith, a specter, and a phantom. I've even been called a vampire because I can only appear solid at night."

"That's what I heard," I told her.

"Heard? You've heard about me? How?"

"Someone we know told us about seeing you many years ago at rock concerts. He said you really stood out. He assumed you were a vampire."

She again sighed, very deeply. I thought I saw tears in her eyes.

"That was a good time, but a very bittersweet time."

"I have to ask you. Were you Pete Ramahi's girlfriend back then?"

"Pete? That psychotic warlock? You're not serious, are you!" Her sudden anger made our rings get brighter. When she noticed that, she let out another big sigh and continued.

"I am so sorry. No. Pete, for some reason, thought I was a kindred spirit. He tried to use his power to seduce me into being one of his family's followers. He did not know what I was. He assumed I was a witch. Also, I was twenty years his senior back then. I was there watching someone else. I was watching my son. Del."

"You're Del's mother?" Bell asked.

"I am. Sorry again. I am not used to socializing. I forgot to introduce myself. I am Tegan Rhees."

"Not Prentiss?" Bell asked.

"I never took my husband's name. I always kept my Welsh name to remind me of my homeland in Wales."

"But we heard you died years ago," I commented. "And his father died not that long ago. Is he still around too?"

"His father is gone, unfortunately. Del thinks his father died a natural death, but I found out recently he was weakened and killed by assassins who, I am sure, were associated with my half sibling con artists, the Wheelers. When Del was only four, another set of assassins had killed me. Whoever the assassins that are hired now are contracted to kill Del as well as his son and daughter. My grandchildren. That is why I made sure the Wheelers could never put out a contract on any of my kind and your kind again. Hopefully."

"What a minute. You said they killed you too?"

She actually smiled at me. "No. They thought they killed me. I did to the assassins what you've seen me do to the Wheelers. Not to brag, but I am a good wizardess."

"Really? I thought Dean was the last wizard around here."

"My brother doesn't know about me yet. I will visit with him once I bring my son Del and my grandchildren back safely. Then we will be the last family of wizards."

"But I thought Del lost most of his powers in the caves here."

"My husband, Ifan, Del's father, was a warlock and trained Del in the arts of incantations and spells. That is what was lost in the caves. I am afraid that was my fault."

"Your fault?" Bell inquired.

"I took their powers away so I could teach them their true magical abilities as wizards. It has taken a long time."

"But why do you only come out at night?" I asked.

"Because of the plague that killed the thousands of wizards, student wizards and their parents... even those without abilities."

"Dean told us about the plague," Bell mentioned.

"He did? Well, when my brother, Dean, was much younger, he wanted to live in your world. He acted like a normal person and went to school in San Francisco. Years later he settled in Volcano. Me, I also wanted to live in your world and used magic to get a job writing for a tabloid newspaper so I would have money to spend in New York. I naturally fell for a young warlock who made an appointment with me. He had outlandish stories of witches in New York that were perfect for the tabloid. Within a month, we wed at the city hall. A year later, Del was born. When he was four is when the evil sorceress committed her atrocity. I was furious. I went back and went after her in anger. We were too well matched. Our magical battle did this to me. I was able to weaken her so the plague could take her. Anyway, our fight weakened me so sunlight could destroy me. I can only come out at night. Ifan thought I died. Del, even though he was a young child, was heartbroken he would never see me again. However, I have been watching over Ifan and Del and protecting them from afar. Yes, during the day, I hide in the darkness of the Black Chasm Cavern. When I'm there and close my eyes, I can see my family, and even you two. That is why your rings glow at different locations here in Volcano. I have been hoping to find and rid the world of these assassins and their owners very soon."

This was a world Bell and I had never heard about before. "I thought the assassins were hired by the Wheelers. They have owners?"

"They do. The Wheelers, and other witch hunters in the past, have hired assassins. This has gone on since medieval times, then completely stopped in the 1960s. It looks as if it has started up again. I am still trying to find out who or what is dispatching these new assassins. I do not yet know."

"Demon?" Bell and I said at the same time.

"I doubt it. When someone wants to hire assassins, this dispatcher somehow knows how to make contact with them. I am hoping I can locate who it is and exterminate the source."

"I really wish you luck," I said, then asked, "So, Del, Dria, and Marty are in your wizard world?"

"You know about that too? Of course. My brother Dean." Tegan laughed. "He never could keep his mouth shut. But he is a good wizard. I am glad you have all become friends with him. Now. I must return to my family. Please be careful. Those new assassins are in hiding somewhere just outside of my reach. They somehow know I am after them. Because you've seen them, they probably know about your abilities too. They may have been told to eliminate you now as well as my family. Oh. And if you run into Reverend Stagnaro, say hello for me."

"Wait. You know the Reverend?"

"He helped me get my grandson Marty to safety before the assassins got him. They were the ones who caused that van to explode. I was with the Reverend on his front steps and was able to transport Marty into the church. Yes, Reverend Stagnaro's shaman power acted as a conduit to his church. As soon as I calmed Marty down, I waved my wand and the three of us came here. Before we left I magically put the sign on the door, Volcano Retreat, as an afterthought. It was really there for Del to find, but he just told me he couldn't ever go back to that... what was it called? Cattle something?

"Catalyst" I answered.

"I had no idea it would appear for the two of you. I'm glad you saw it and were able to come and help my brother, son, and grandchildren. Now, I'm sorry again, but I really must leave before the morning twilight. I don't want to stay away from my family too long. They are not well trained as wizards yet. Now, I must leave and head back to the darkness of the cave… in my time."

Tegan didn't move from the chair. She smiled at us and pulled out a wand, a branch similar to Dean's, waved it, and disappeared right in front of us. It made our rings glow and gave us both a slight shock.

Bell and I looked at each other. Both of us shrugged, took off our clothes and hopped back in bed. We kissed, then immediately fell asleep, like we were willed to do so.

We both woke up at 7:00 am, on the dot. We stretched, kissed good morning, and got up to take our showers. We felt incredibly refreshed. It had to be Tegan's doing.

By 8:00 we were in the hotel's dining room. A breakfast buffet had been set up with three heated and covered chafing pans. One pan had scrambled eggs. Another had both bacon and link sausages. The third had hash browns. There was also a covered circular pan with hot oatmeal. Other unheated pans had fruit, and pastries, like croissants, eclairs, and glazed donut holes. Small packages of cereal were stacked on a table next to pump thermoses with milk, orange juice, coffee and hot water for tea.

I got a plate and filled it with selections from the hot chafing pans, along with some fruit. After I set it on our table, I went back and got a cup of coffee.

Bell did the same, but also grabbed a croissant and a glass of orange juice.

We were just starting to eat when Granny and Gwyn came in. They both got oatmeal and hot water for tea. Granny grabbed an herbal tea bag from a basket, and Gwyn selected black tea. She appeared to be deep in thought.

"Is Garrett up?" I asked. "We can bring another chair over for him."

"He got up early and left," Granny replied. "He's heading back to San Francisco. He has a meeting with his attorney tomorrow to draw up a contract for me to sign. I'll be purchasing his house on the price we agreed on in a few weeks. I'll be paying cash directly to Garrett."

"Granny. I never asked. Where is Garrett's house?"

"It's in a beautiful neighborhood in the Sea Cliff area, just above the Richmond District. Garrett has owned it since it was built in the 1920s."

"The 1920s?" Bell questioned. "How old is Garrett?"

"Oh, he is my age." Granny chuckled. "Now children, don't ask me how old I am. That's not nice."

"By the way, Granny, we had a visitor drop in around three in the morning."

"A visitor at that time? Who?"

"A tall pale woman. The one who killed the Wheelers."

"Oh my gods and goddesses! Is she dangerous?"

"We thought so at first. Del mentioned seeing her when he was young and in that band with Pete Ramahi. He thought she was a Ramahi follower. He also thought she might be a vampire. Not so. Granny, she was quite pleasant. She's really Del's mother. Dean's sister."

Granny's mouth was open, but she was speechless.

Gwyn spoke up. "Interesting. Hmm. Del never told me. I couldn't see that in his memory."

"Gwyn, can you read Dean's memory?" I asked.

"No, I cannot. Why?"

"Del and his children are wizards. As Tegan... yes, that is her name. Tegan Rhees. Anyway, she told us that Dean, her, Del, and his children are the last family of wizards."

"Did I hear my name mentioned?" Dean came in smiling and walked up to our table.

I looked up at him. "Dean, we had a visit last night from your sister, Tegan."

His smile faded. He pulled a chair over from another table and sat down with a thud. "That cannot be. She is dead. She is... uh... really?"

"Yes. She has been living in that wizard place you mentioned. She's been there all these years. She has been watching over Del and his children. Her grandchildren."

It looked like Dean was in shock. He finally shook his head. "Is she responsible for the murders?"

"Yes, but for a reason. It was the Wheelers who contacted someone to get the assassins. They have the ability to trace the locations of witches and warlocks, and I'm sure, wizards. These two assassins, who Bell and I saw at Del's house a week or so ago, are out to kill Del and his children. They may be after us now too. They have disappeared and even Tegan can't locate them. I'm sure they are hiding and still somewhere in or around Volcano."

"Del is okay? Dria and Marty are okay? They must be with Tegan. Yes? That is why I could not fully pick up Del's whereabouts. I got little hints of his presence… I still do. But the feelings are fleeting."

"Tegan has started training them to be wizards. She told us they have always had wizard genes. But through Del's father, they also have his warlock genes. That is what they always thought they were."

"I have a wizard family?" Dean leaned back in his chair and his smile returned. "I had hopes. Now I must see them."

"Please wait," I said. "Tegan wants them to stay there for a while until we can make sure the assassins are gone. Maybe terminated. She's looking into it. We're going to help to try to find some clues in our world here. You want to help?"

"Of course. Anything to get my family back together."

"Good. And remember, Tegan has been watching."

Chapter 16

Before we finished our breakfasts, Dean left to go home. He wanted to prepare for the return of his sister and for a possible encounter with the assassins. No sooner had he left than Paul, the Reverend Stagnaro, arrived and sat with us. I couldn't read anything in his eyes. Now I knew why.

"I understand you got a visit last night from Tegan."

Granny looked at him askance. "You know Tegan?"

I told Granny, "I didn't get to tell you that part yet. Go ahead, Paul."

"Yes. I've known Tegan for quite a while. I knew her late husband too. I am sorry I kept it from you. It was for Tegan's sake. I was there in Santa Cruz when young Marty disappeared, and his van blew up. That explosion was caused by those assassins. I helped Tegan get Marty out of the van just before it incinerated."

"You helped Tegan?" Granny asked. "Are you also a wizard?"

"No, I am not. As I told Charles, my grandfather on my father's side of the family was a Miwok shaman. I have some of those abilities, not quite as many as Mister Blue here though. My main ability is to work as a conduit from one place to another. In this case, Tegan's magic helped me move Marty from his van to my church. Now. The other reason I came by is that the assassins, those two who arrived with the Wheelers, checked out of the Inn and drove off this morning, quite fast in their Porsche, heading out of town. They weren't driving west toward Sutter Creek, but south, toward Black Chasm Cavern."

"I don't trust that they are really gone," Bell said. "I bet they are going into hiding, maybe in that cave thinking we may not go in or can't locate them. Or... maybe they're looking for a way to get to Tegan."

"We should try. That could give us an advantage. We certainly outnumber them. Granny, let's get ready to go on a short road trip to Black Chasm and see if their Porsche is there."

"What if we need to go into the cavern to confront the assassins?" Bell asked.

"I'll bring all the protective gear I brought, just in case," Granny replied.

"Granny, I just thought of something. If it's possible that natural caves might erase or lessen our powers, even if we're protected, will we be able to use our powers?"

"Oh my gods and goddesses. You're right, dear Charles. I was assuming with our powers we would be able to combat those killers if we came across them in the cave. Maybe Dean..."

Gwyn interrupted Granny. "Freesia is missing. I cannot

psychically contact her."

"Oh no," Bell and Granny said together. Bell asked, "Was she with you this morning?"

"No, she was not. She went out last night to spy on the assassins over at the Inn. She was trying to get close to their room to hear what their plans were. The last she told me was that the assassins never spoke but nodded like they were in contact with someone on the outside. She could not hear any telepathic messages from them. That was close to midnight. I fell asleep thinking Freesia would be back soon. When I awoke, she had not returned. I tried to contact her and could not. I am worried."

"Do you think she snuck into their car?" I asked. "Maybe she followed them into the cave. I hope she's alright. Come on. Let's go."

It took over thirty minutes for everyone to get ready and pile into our van. Dean had walked back down to the hotel and joined us. He was holding four wands, oak twigs of various lengths, all with a pair of short branches on the ends forming a V. "I just made these. They are for Del, Dria, and Marty. I hope to personally give them to them soon."

It was nearly 11:00 when we arrived at Black Chasm Cavern. According to the sign at the entrance, its Winter hours were 10am to 4pm. Another hand-lettered sign below it said temporarily closed for the holidays. The gate was open, so we drove in.

And there was the Porsche. No other cars were there. No guides. No security. That seemed odd to us at first, then realized the assassins, or their dispatcher, probably had something to do with it.

Bell pointed to the front door of the gift shop building. It was open. "This looks as if they're inviting us to find them. Have any of you thought this might be a trap?"

"Let me take care of that," Dean volunteered. "I will go in first." He took out his wand, got out of the van, and waved it in a circle. "Stay in the car for at least five minutes. I have put a shield up over your car to protect you if they run out and try to get at you. I know you can do protection spells, but mine totally seals you in. I will come back and remove the shield when it is safe. Okay. Here I go."

Dean stepped up on the front porch. He had his wand up for protection and went through the open door.

The lights were off in the building. It was still fairly bright from the windows and skylights. No one was inside. Dean noticed a couple of security cameras in the eaves, but the lenses had been changed to point straight up. He also noticed the back door leading to the cavern's entrance was also open. He walked toward the back, wand at the ready.

Before he reached the door, Freesia came running in past him and out the front door. She looked panicked. Dean glanced back out the back door and thought he heard footsteps running. Dean closed the door and latched it just as one of the assassins ran headfirst into it, knocking himself back. He fell down and rolled partway down the incline toward the cave entrance. Dean ran out the front door.

The shield was still up on the van and Freesia was scratching at it trying to get to Gwyn. Dean waved his wand and the shield fell, letting Bell open the sliding side door for Freesia. She immediately leapt into Gwyn's lap. I could hear her crying.

Dean jumped in and said we should go. Quickly. I didn't think twice. I started the van and tore out of the parking area, throwing gravel that hit and pock-marked the Porsche and setting off its car alarm.

I sped around the circular drive and headed toward the gated entrance by the Volcano Pioneer Road. The metal gate was now closed and padlocked. Was someone on the outside trying to keep us in? I skidded to a stop nearly hitting the gate. Dean jumped out, reached over the gate, and tapped the padlock with his wand. It dropped, and he opened the gate then jumped back in the van. I accelerated out the gate but stopped just before the road. This time Bell jumped out, closed the gate, and relocked the padlock. She held on to the padlock and I could see she was using one of her powers to permanently lock the gate. The assassins would not be able to open it.

Bell jumped back in. "I can hear that Porsche of theirs heading this way. Let's hurry away from here."

As I accelerated again, heading out the driveway, I noticed in my side view mirror the black Porsche speeding toward us. I was paying attention to driving and couldn't look as I turned onto the main road. The others were watching out the back window to see if the assassins could get through the gate and follow us. That Porsche could overtake us in a heartbeat.

I heard Dean, Granny, and Bell say "Wow!"

"What? What?" I said with my foot still pushed hard on the gas pedal.

"They hit that immovable gate hard," Dean said. "They must have thought they could smash through it. We saw pieces of car fly out in the street behind us. Good job, Bell."

"Thanks. Now, Charles, you can slow down."

Chapter 17

By the time we returned to the hotel and headed for the bar, all our adrenaline had abated, and we plopped down into chairs at a vacant table. Gwyn went to her room to sooth Freesia. I had never seen a cat cry, but knowing that she was once human, made it seem natural.

I was leaning back in my chair and started shaking.

"Charles, dear, are you okay?" Granny asked. "Oh my gods and goddesses. Look at your ring. You too, Bell."

Both rings were shining so much they were almost blinding. We put our hands over them so any others, like the bartender and miners at the bar, wouldn't notice them.

Bell was shaking too. "It feels like an electrical shock. More so than I've experienced before. You too?"

"Me too. I also hear a buzzing in my ear. No… It's a voice."

"I hear it too," Bell said almost too loudly. "It's Tegan!"

"Shush, children. Keep your voices down. Speak telepathically."

"Sorry, Granny. Tegan is speaking to us."

"What is she saying?"

"Shh. Tell you in a minute."

Three minutes later, our rings stopped shining. Tegan was gone from our heads.

"Holy cow, Granny. Everyone. Tegan was in the total darkness of the cavern and knew all that transpired. And also knew Freesia was spying on the assassins and was sorry she scared her when her image appeared. When Freesia ran out, it alerted the assassins, and they chased her. She said the rest we know. The chase and the two assassins dying in that crash. The gate actually beheaded them. But she also said she knows that another assassin or two will replace the dead ones almost immediately. She said to be aware and careful."

"How does she know all that?" I asked telepathically then whispered aloud to Dean. "How does she know all that?"

"Know what?" Dean questioned.

"Sorry. We were talking telepathically," I quietly related what Tegan told me and Bell.

"Ah yes. Well. Magic. I remember my sister being able to close her eyes and envision walking around, viewing things, and even speaking, anywhere. Well, anywhere within a ten-mile radius. But she must have made an appearance in the cave's darkness. She was… can even create magic remotely."

"But Dean, why did her vision appear in the cavern?" Bell asked him this time. "I thought she hid deeper in the darkness."

"She said she was looking for the assassin's dispatcher. She must have used her magic to follow those assassins. I do not know how she does it, but she can ghost her way into places from where she hides or from the wizarding realm. Something I could not do. She was probably there to help us if we needed it. I am sure she was watching everything that happened."

While listening to Dean, we didn't notice that Gwyn came in. She was pulling her small, wheeled suitcase behind her.

"I must take my leave of you wonderful people. Freesia has been through a lot and is not feeling well right now, mentally and physically. I need to take her home to nurse her back to health. Yana, please come see me when you get back to Santa Cruz. Charles, Bell, you are welcome too."

"We will all come, Gwyn, and work to get Freesia back to her human form. I'm really hoping between the three of us we can reverse her curse."

Gwyn and Granny gave each other a big hug. Gwyn gave us all quick hugs all around, then headed out to her VW bug. Granny went out to wave goodbye then came back in a seat back down at our table. "Freesia is asleep in the back seat. I am worried about her. She has been a cat for over twenty years now. That is very very old for a cat. If we can't change her back, she may die soon. We have to try to help her as soon as we can."

We all agreed. Dean even said he wished he could help, but he needs to get his family back together and make sure the assassin threat is over.

"I appreciate all you have done to help," Dean said. "Now that I know that Del and his children are okay, and my sister is alive, you do not have to stick around, unless you want to. I know Christmas is coming up. You probably want to get home to celebrate."

"We don't really celebrate Christmas," Granny said. "We kind of fake it, to try to look normal to the neighbors, but we don't give presents or do the church thing."

"Ah. Wizards... well, this wizard is the same. I usually put up a few lights outside my house to make it look festive for the locals. Sorry to say, but Christmas Day is just another day to me."

"Well, contrary to what you all believe, I like celebrating Christmas," I told them. "Remember, my first seventeen years was in a regular middle-class home in Sunnyvale. I always looked forward to Christmas with the festivities and the music. Bell, Granny, what say we head home tomorrow morning. I really would like to put up a tree."

"Dean, will you be okay on your own?" Granny asked.

"Oh yes. I have been on my own for a very long time."

Dean forced a smile. It occurred to me he hadn't been very happy to be alone for so long. I was hoping that when his sister and the others returned, he would be much happier. Now I was reconsidering if we should really leave in the morning. I liked Dean. I would like to learn more about his wizarding and his world. *Well, maybe another time.*

After breakfast the next morning we went to our rooms and began packing. Granny was ready long before Bell and I were. After all, she could just toss everything of hers in her carpet bag satchel and it always came out clean, pressed, and orderly. Bell and I didn't have that convenience. We still had to carefully fold and put our clothes and toiletries in her suitcase and my backpack.

"Bell, before we go, we should go over to the Inn and see if Paul

Stagnaro is still there. I want to find out if he'll be in Santa Cruz soon or if he's going to work in Sutter Creek. I'd like to talk to him and find out more about him."

"I'd like to talk to him too. He was interesting. Yes, let's take a walk over there to see him before we leave. We've got until eleven before we have to check out."

Bell and I walked the short distance to the Inn and noticed the Wheeler's black Mercedes was back and parked in front of it. We both wondered who drove it off and who brought it back. The white one was gone this time. Nicolas Wheeler's girlfriend, Rhea, must have driven off in it.

"Charles, should we do something about that car? There's going to be questions asked why it was left here and where the owner is. Especially since they had signed the register when they checked in."

"Let's go in and ask the young woman at the desk if they did check out or not."

We walked in the front door and up to the counter and stood behind Reverend Stagnaro who was just checking out himself.

"Ah. Reverend. Glad we caught you. Bell and I were just coming over to say goodbye."

"That is very nice of you," he said as he turned and shook Bell's hand then mine.

"Are you heading back to Santa Cruz?" I asked.

"Not until after the holidays. I'll be staying in Sutter Creek for a few days to help serve the Christmas dinner. Also, I need to be close enough for Tegan to contact me if I'm needed there. Well, it was nice meeting you and the others. You do good work. Now I must do some of God's work."

"Before you go, Reverend, have you noticed the Wheelers' car is still out front?"

"But not for long. Dean helped me sneak out the Wheelers' suitcases and we found a second set of keys and found the pink slip in the glove box. Evidently, they paid cash for that car. There's no loan out on it. I'll drive this ostentatious vehicle to my church in Sutter Creek and park it there for the time being. At least until I can sell it to help fund my missions."

"Sounds like you and Dean have a handle on it. Except…"

"Except?"

"Are the Wheelers still signed in on the register?"

"Oh. That. Yes and no. Still signed in, but the Inn thinks they skipped out. Also, there is a lot of talk here about that 'accident'." The Reverend used air quotes. "That other couple, those assassins, were also still signed in as Mister and Missus Smyth. I am sure that is not their real name. The sheriff's department is just saying it was an unfortunate accident and don't plan to investigate any further on it. Well, Dean's abilities helped quiet it down too. Now, I really must take my leave. Goodbye, you two."

He shook our hands again and walked out. We saw him put his suitcase in the back seat, and he hopped in and started the Mercedes. The throaty sound from the exhaust made it sound more like a race car than a luxury sedan. We heard the sound echoing through the hills for several minutes after he left.

"Well, Bell. Let's head back to the hotel, get Granny, and check out. I want to get home so we can decompress and relax."

"I hope we can. However, lover, I don't think this is over yet."

Chapter 18

It took nearly six hours to get home. Driving time would normally be around four hours, but we had a long leisurely lunch at a Denny's in Stockton before heading back to the coast.

As we drove through my foggy Pleasure Point neighborhood, I was noticing all the Christmas decorations on many of the houses. I felt a little nostalgic thinking about my youth and Christmas in Sunnyvale with my parents. Then felt angry at what had happened to them and the home I grew up in. Not a very Christmas-like feeling.

But that feeling was temporary. I sighed with relief as we pulled into my driveway. We were home.

It was nearly 5pm when we finished unpacking. I asked Granny if she wanted to stay a few more days and spend Christmas with us. She looked at me askance. "Now you know I've never celebrated these holidays. My real celebrations are the Spring and Fall equinoxes."

"I know that Granny. But Bell and I would like to take you out for dinner on Christmas Eve. The Crow's Nest restaurant has a special dinner that night. They do have vegetarian selections."

"Well, that sounds okay. Okay. Sure, dear ones. I'll stick around for a couple more days. I can visit with Gwyn."

Bell and I were worn out, and I thought Granny would be worse off. However, the next day she woke up at her regular time at six. Bell and I slept until eight. By the time we walked into the kitchen in our bathrobes, Granny had already made coffee for us. She was sitting at the kitchen table sipping her specially brewed tea using her own concoction.

"You children finally woke up? You still look half asleep. I made coffee for you. Hope I did it right."

I poured two cups and took a sip from mine. "Not bad, Granny." I couldn't add milk as I normally did because the half empty milk carton had gone bad. Since we had been away for a while, our refrigerator was a little bare.

"Say, after Bell and I get cleaned up, I'll go to the store and pick up a few things for our meals here. Do you need anything?"

"I could use some dried cremini mushrooms for my tea. I'm almost out. Oh. And a bottle of dry sherry. If you can't get a Spanish amontillado, I can get by with a local Christian Brothers or Gallo. Try to get the Spanish one if you can."

"Sherry?" Bell asked. "I don't remember you ever drinking sherry."

"Drink? Heavens no. I really don't like to drink sherry by itself.

I use it in one of my teas. The Spanish one does make a better brew." Granny said that last sentence with a half-smile and a little twinkle in her eyes. *Sure. Just like my dad used to like coffee Royale, he would pour brandy in his coffee, smile and say it improved the taste. Ah. Another old memory.*

After a quick breakfast of frozen waffles crisped up in the toaster, Bell and I took a nice long, warm, and loving shower together. Our shower took way too long, and the water heater ran out of hot water. Time to dry off and get dressed.

Bell stayed and talked to Granny while I went to Shopper's Corner and moseyed around with a shopping cart getting items for our meals… and for Granny's brews.

At the meat counter, I reached up to grab a number and moved back to wait for my number to come up when I felt a hand on my shoulder. I started.

"Gwyn!"

"Good morning, Charles. I knew you would be here. I am glad. I needed to shop for victuals too. Oh. You seem to have a glow about you." Gwyn chuckled. "I cannot tell, but is Yana at your house too?"

"Yes. She is staying with us for a few days. I'm taking her and Bell out for Christmas Eve dinner."

"You celebrate that… thing?"

"Not anymore. I…"

"Say no more. I know of your background. You did celebrate this holiday in your youth. I… I am so sorry to have brought that up."

Gwyn could tell my mind drifted back to my parents during Christmas. I had drifted off thinking about that. I caught myself when Gwyn stopped talking.

"I'm sorry Gwyn. My mind went elsewhere."

"Dear Charles. I get the feeling you and Bell will be going elsewhere one of these days. Oh. I should not have said that. Never mind."

Gwyn seemed to see something in my future. I thought future readings of our kind were not possible. I was told that. Now. True or false?

"Please tell Yana to come see me on my boat. I do need to talk to her."

She sped off pushing her shopping cart to the registers to check out. I started to follow to ask her how Freesia was, but my number was called at the meat counter. *Damn!*

A half hour later as I was carrying a grocery bag into the house, I felt a little pinch on my ring finger.

"Charles!" Bell said, with a nervous look on her face. "My ring is pinching. Is yours too?"

I sat the bag down on the counter. "I just noticed it as I came in. They're not glowing though. Why the pinch?"

Granny got up out from the sofa, came over to us and held our left hands and looked at the rings. "Charles, your ring has done that before. Bell, this may be new to you. As I recall from your mother, Bell, that pinching warns of an impending event. Good or bad. What it is, we will not know until it happens."

"Maybe it has to do with my running into Gwyn at Shopper's Corner. She mentioned that Bell and I will be going somewhere one of these days, then said she shouldn't have said that. Hmm." I paused in thought. "Anyway, Granny, she said she wants to talk to you. No, she didn't say what it was about."

"Can you drive me over there and drop me off?"

I agreed. And after I finished unloading the groceries, Granny had changed into the same flannel shirt and jeans she had on in Volcano and was ready to go.

Bell wanted to stay in the house and write in her journal about all that had happened, to have a record of the type of incantations and magic that took place. Granny had written many journals throughout her life and careers, as had Bell's mother, Constance. Bell wanted to continue the tradition.

Granny and I climbed into the van, and I drove her to the yacht harbor. I dropped her off at the dock where Gwyn's boat was moored.

I got out with Granny and walked up to the gate. Again, it unlocked and opened right in front of us. Granny pulled me down to her height and gave me a light kiss on the cheek. "I may be here for quite a while. Don't worry about me. I'll be fine with my friend Gwyn."

"If you're sure, Granny. Let me know when you'll need a ride back."

"I will. You will know when."

Chapter 19

When I got back to the house, Bell was still writing in her journal. She put her pen down when I came up to her, and she pulled me down to sit by her. She put her arms around me and gave me a full, tongue-active kiss that made me think about things other than our mystery concerns. *Oh, well. Short lived.*

"Charles, love. As I was writing in my journal, I was thinking about why the Wheelers have always wanted to destroy our kind and also why Dean's family became the target."

"You remember when we visited Del's house and the Wheelers, and those others were there? When we were outside the house, we heard them loudly talking and they considered Del and his kids to be like us. I think they also thought Dean was a warlock too and may have been targeting him as such. They did not know he is really a wizard."

"I am worried that more assassins could be dispatched to try to finish the job the others failed at. Maybe Gwyn knows. Maybe that is why Yana was asked to meet with her."

"I can't feel that one way or another. Bell, you seem to have picked up some type of psychic ability recently. I wish I had some too. You know, like Gwyn."

"Maybe you do, Charles. What about your grandfather's spirit? Your medicine bag?"

"Peter Red Feather has only visited me during heavy-duty healing spells to guide me. I haven't used my medicine bag for anything else other than simple healing and calming spells. We can do much of that with our own witch and warlock abilities."

"What about your grandfather's Ohlone writings? I know a lot of it is symbolic, but you did tell me that he wrote in the old language phonetically many times. Why don't you get his journal and see what else you might be able to do?"

I went into our bedroom and once again opened my 'empty' trunk and pulled out the thick deer leather bound journal that had belonged to my grandfather. I brought it into the living room and set it on the coffee table.

"Wish I could read that like you can, Charles. That's beautiful leather. And the writing and symbols are gorgeous."

"They are, aren't they. Well, let's see."

As I opened the journal several pages flipped to each side exposing just what we were talking about: psychic abilities. It related to how medicine men, shamans, can view current and past events in their minds. I had never seen this in this journal before. I thought I had read the whole thing. It was as if new writings had appeared since last reading it.

"Bell. This was not in here before. I believe grandfather somehow added just what we need. I'm astounded."

I related to Bell just what I read, then read it again to myself.

"Okay. It tells me what to do. Grandfather is telling me what to do."

I pulled my medicine bag out from under my denim shirt, held it in my left hand, closed my eyes and said in Ohlone what the journal said to say.

Immediately, I could see, on the back of my eyelids, Granny and Gwyn and a sleeping Freesia, curled up on a pillow. Then I saw the inside of the boat weaving from side to side. Gwyn's boat was out in the bay. It was heading west toward the open ocean while the two of them sat talking and drinking tea. I could see no one else there. *Who was piloting the boat?*

I opened my eyes.

"Bell. It worked. Granny and Gwyn are on her boat and heading out to sea. I'll try again later and see if I can tell where they're heading. I think Gwyn's boat is driving itself. Magic you think?"

"The only real magic practitioners we now know are Dean and Tegan. But we left him in Volcano. And Tegan's in her daytime hiding. Anyway, I doubt either of them would know how to pilot a boat."

"I wonder if I can use my medicine bag to envision Dean. Hmm. Let me read grandfather's journal a little more. Uh… there is something else here I don't remember. Grandfather says here that psychic visions do not work on magical beings. I seem to remember Gwyn saying something like that."

"Beings? Plural? Makes me wonder if there were others with wizard or sorceress powers when your grandfather wrote that. Maybe other shaman you think?"

"Uh… Bell. Grandfather's here."

"Where? I don't see him."

"He's sitting right across from us in my recliner."

"Is he talking to you?"

"No. He… he's signing. Talking with his hands. He is saying… Medicine. Bag. Need. More… no. New. Uh… ashes. He's saying my medicine bag needs, I think, new filling. New ashes."

"Really? I thought it just worked all the time."

"Now he's saying… Read. Journal. Last. Page. I. Will. Talk. Again. Grandfather? Wow. He's gone."

"Check the last page. What was he referring to?"

"Another writing I don't remember being here. Grandfather must have added it just now. It's directions on recharging a medicine bag. Wow. Who'da thunk it."

"What do you need to do?"

"First, I need to find some vellum. Real calf or goat vellum. Maybe at one of the art stores in town. I think the only one open right now is Lenz Arts. It's nearly one. Let's have a little lunch then take a ride over there."

I quickly made a couple of quesadillas out of some tortillas and cheddar I got at the store this morning. A half hour later, we were in the van on the way to the art store.

I had no luck at the art store. They only had fake vellum made from paper. The clerk gave us a good suggestion to check at the tannery.

Salz Tannery was only a half mile from the art store. At the far end of the tannery and in the back was The Dead Cow, the store where you could buy full or partial plain and dyed leather skins, supplies and tools for working leather, and leather gifts, like wallets, key chains, and coasters, all with the Salz logo on them. I asked about calf vellum. The clerk new everything I needed to know.

"We do have a few pieces of goat vellum. Not much call for that anymore. Real calf vellum that was used in the old days hasn't been available for maybe decades. Would you like the goat? I need to get it out of the storage room. Excuse me a second."

"Charles." Bell gently grabbed my arm. "I'm getting a weird feeling something is happening. Look. Our rings are glowing. Cover yours. Quickly. The clerk is coming back."

I put my left hand in my pocket to keep my ring out of sight. Bell did the same.

"I have two twelve by sixteen sheets left. My boss back there said you could have them both for the price of one. Fifteen dollars, plus tax."

"Then I'll take them both." With my right hand I reached in my back pocket and pulled out my wallet then wondered how I was going to hold it to pull a twenty out of it. I turned away from the clerk and pulled my left hand out of my pocket. My ring wasn't glowing now. *Whew*! "Here's a twenty. Keep the change."

The clerk thanked us as she rolled up the vellum and put it in a cardboard tube.

When Bell and I got back into the van, she said, "Lately, our rings have only glowed when Tegan was around. Could she be here now?"

"I don't know. Our rings glowed several months ago when you found yours in the San Francisco Victorian basement. We were not aware of Tegan then. There must be another reason for our rings to glow."

"Charles. Please use your shaman ability again when we get home. Check on Yana, your Granny, please. I feel something is terribly wrong, and our rings are telling us.

Chapter 20

I drove home as quickly as traffic allowed and rushed into the house.

I dropped the tube with the vellum on the kitchen table, then sat down on the sofa. Bell came up beside me, gave me a kiss on the cheek and nodded for me to go ahead. She sat down next to me and kept quiet.

I again held onto my medicine bag, closed my eyes, and recited a psychic spell in Ohlone. And, again, on the back of my eyelids, I could see… I could barely see Granny. I tried looking beyond and thought I could see another figure. It was a very blurry silhouette and looked masculine. It couldn't be Gwyn. She was tall but not that tall. I couldn't see Gwyn or Freesia. Also, the boat, if that was where Granny still was, did not seem to be moving. I could tell nothing else.

"Bell. Now I'm really worried. Everything was blurry. I'm sure I saw Granny, but I couldn't make out a figure behind her. It looked too big to be Gwyn."

"Charles, your grandfather basically told you to recharge your medicine bag. Maybe you'll have better… uh… reception? Check the journal."

The last page on the journal had changed again. Grandfather's spirit had been busy. Now it had directions on what to write on a piece of vellum, how to prepare it, how to burn it, and how to put the new ashes in the medicine bag. Seemed simple enough. I hoped.

"Oh crud, Bell. If Granny is off with Gwyn somewhere, I'll have to cancel tomorrow's Christmas Eve dinner reservation at the Crow's Nest. Damn. I also wanted to get a small tree to put up today."

"Fix your medicine bag first. Maybe after you get a better vision of Yana, and we know she's alright, we can run over to the hardware store and see if they have a little fake tree we can get. I do wish I could spend a quiet Christmas with you."

I didn't tell Bell, but I also wanted to find a little gift for her to open on Christmas morning. After all, this was our first real holiday season as a couple.

Following my grandfather's directions, I wrote and drew Ohlone words and figures that represented several generations of shaman and put the vellum in the oven to dry the thin leather. I then started a fire in my fireplace. I folded the vellum, so it was barely four inches square and placed it in a fine wire strainer with a long handle that I used for draining pasta. Once the fire was at its hottest, I held the strainer, with an oven mitt, over the fire. Within ten minutes the vellum was ash.

I had tried to open my medicine bag once before when I first got it, but to no avail. I was only able to drop a little ash out of it. This time, with grandfather's instructions, the medicine bag opened without a problem. I was told to empty the old ashes into the fire so any remaining spiritual remnants would rise up the chimney to the sky. I filled the medicine bag with the new ashes and sealed it up, retying the cord I wear around my neck.

"Okay, Bell. What say I try this out. Let's sit down."

I repeated all I had to do to try to get another vision of Granny.

It all became clear again. Seeing the vision on the inside of my eyelids was like watching television up close. I saw Granny and Gwyn. Freesia was still sleeping on her pillow. Granny and Gwyn didn't look as talkative as they were the first time I saw them. They looked awfully serious in fact. They looked up as if looking at me. However, it wasn't me they were looking at. Someone else was now coming into the scene. A man. He did not look as clear as Granny and Gwyn. Kind of ghostly. He turned around and I was sure he looked straight at me. Dean. Why is he on Gwyn's boat? How did he get there? He pointed at me and motioned for me to come. He knew I was watching. I could not hear anything anyone said, but I could see Dean mouth 'Volcano' to me then turned back to talk to the others. I opened my eyes.

"Bell! We have to go back to Volcano!"

After quickly repacking our bags and throwing together a couple of cheese sandwiches to eat on the way, we drove off. It was late afternoon, nearly 4:30, and we knew it would be dark by six.

Bell and I were quiet and deep in thought for nearly a hundred miles. Bell was the first to break the silence. "I'm sorry our first Christmas together is not working out the way you wanted. Maybe we can enjoy Christmas morning by the tree in the hotel lobby and sip coffee, or something stronger, in front of the fireplace."

"That would be nice. Maybe the hotel restaurant will have some good holiday meals." I sighed. "I don't understand why Granny took off with Gwyn without letting us know."

"She must have had a good reason. By any chance did you see where Gwyn's boat was headed?"

"No. I wasn't able to that last time I saw them… and Dean. Jeez. He must have used his magic to appear on her boat. I really don't think it was his real self. He seemed to float into the galley where Granny and Gwyn were sitting. He looked like a ghost."

"He had to be projecting his image somehow. Charles, I would really like to know more about wizards. My mother never talked about them, and I don't think I remember any coming into the Mystic Eye when I worked there. But maybe they were all gone by then."

"Probably. Anyway, I would like to talk to Dean more when this whole situation is resolved."

We kept quiet for another fifty miles then began talking about when we could move back to San Francisco and about Granny's purchase of Garrett's house. My contractor had called before we left and gave me an update on the progress. He said my Victorian should be finished by Spring, and Bell's 1930s era Telegraph Hill home's restoration should be finished sometime later by the end the Summer, if the subcontractors didn't get backed up working on other buildings damaged by the earthquake.

Bell had lovingly kept her hand on my leg the whole drive. We headed south on Highway 99 and finally reached the turnoff that headed up the Sierra foothills and into the gold rush country and Sutter Creek. It had been getting cloudier when we left 99 and now a light cold rain was falling.

It was 8:30 when we pulled in front of the Saint George Hotel. There was no parking in front, and we were worried the hotel was booked up. We pulled around the corner and into a parking space on the side street. The streets were wet, but the rain had stopped. It felt so cold I thought it might snow.

Bell and I got out of the van and walked around the corner and into the hotel lobby. Ah. The restaurant was full, and the bar was too. We went up to the counter. The same woman in an old-fashioned gingham dress was behind the desk. She recognized us.

"So glad you are back. Would you like your same room?"

"Yes please. We saw all these cars and were worried you were booked up."

"Almost. Several of the cars out there belong to the volunteer fire department and some of our locals. It is a community meeting about a suspicious fire that happened yesterday."

"Fire? Forest fire?" I asked.

"No. It was Dean Prentiss's house."

Chapter 21

Oh my God! Dean's house! How did that happen? Did Dean die? Was that really his ghost on Gwyn's boat?

"What happened?" I asked the lady behind the counter.

"That's what they're talking about in there." She pointed to the restaurant and bar. "So far, no one has figured out what caused the fire or how it started. They know it wasn't electrical. Dean had new wiring put in four or five years ago. They also know it didn't start at his fireplace. He didn't have a fire burning at the time. They really don't know yet."

"How about Dean? Is he okay?"

"They're talking about that too. Dean wasn't there. He hasn't been seen."

Bell and I looked at each other and I spoke to her telepathically. "Let's check in and get our stuff to our room then go for a walk. It's *awfully late, but I want to walk up to Dean's place and see if we can figure anything out. Maybe we can determine if Dean is okay. If he's missing, he might be with Tegan."*

I turned back to the lady behind the counter who had turned the register book around to us. "Go ahead and sign in again, please. Welcome back Mister and Missus Blue. Here is your key."

We thanked her and headed to the restaurant and bar. Bell gave me a gentle punch on my shoulder and whispered, "Missus Blue? Did we get married without me knowing it?"

As we walked into the bar, we noticed that the same old miners were there again sharing a bottle and drinking whiskey. They didn't look like they were part of the meeting. The others in the room seemed to have been drinking for a while just like the miners. The room was warm from all the bodies and smelled like stale beer and sweat.

It was a cacophony of voices. Everyone was trying to talk at once. Whoever was supposed to be moderating was probably too drunk to care. Through the noise we could barely make out some random words, several slurred, like fire, explosion, white light, and Dean's name mentioned a lot. Someone loudly commented about a crazy old man and an insurance scam. Another angrily said that idea is stupid. Bell and I watched as the insurance scam talking guy got up and attempted to punch his critic who started to pull a revolver out of his holster. A few others got up to separate them. The gun slipped back in its holster. Some others just laughed. Bell and I thought we'd better get out of the way of the door in case some wild west shooting started.

"Jeez, Bell. There's some drunken animosity and weird vibes in there. Let's go get our luggage and go to our room to get settled in. Then head

up to Dean's house."

When we left the hotel, the meeting was breaking up. The only people remaining were the miners at the bar who were joined by the guy with the gun and the guy who tried to hit him. Laughing. Odd couple.

It was after 9pm when we began walking up toward Dean's house. The temperature felt like it was close to freezing. We could see our breath as we panted walking quickly up the incline to his home. Fortunately, we had our thick down coats on. We also brought along a pair of flashlights and umbrellas, in case of rain, which stopped for now., or of snow.

Dean's house actually looked intact. The windows were broken, and the door looked like it was forced open by the fire fighters. We walked up to the front porch and shined our flashlights inside. Yes, it was gutted. Yet the structure of the house looked in good shape. Maybe Dean had some kind of protection on it. After all, usually an old dry wood house like this would have quickly burned to the ground.

Bell put her hand on the door frame and closed her eyes. I noticed she took a quick intake of breath. She let go and came back to stand by me and put her arm through mine, shaking her head.

"Are you okay, Bell? What did you see?"

"Assassin. I'm sure it was a single assassin who torched the house. Dean was here, but not here now."

"You remember hearing someone at that meeting saying something about white light? Maybe it's like what happened to Marty, Del's son?"

"So these assassins have some kind of power. Are they like us? Or are they wizards of some sort, like Dean?"

"Whatever they are, they are evil. However, they are also mortal and can be killed as we found out at the cavern."

"Hmm. Charles, I wonder how many of them there are, and where can we find the source. Maybe they'll keep coming until whoever they're after is eliminated."

"I know. Not a pleasant thought, but I've been thinking about that too. Bell, love. Let's go on back to the hotel. It's freezing out here."

It was much warmer in the lobby. The fireplace had a couple of oak logs burning that put out a very comfortable heat. All the seats except two were filled with Christmas visitors.

"Hey, lover, let's get a couple of glasses of wine and relax in front of the fire. It's been a long day."

"Great idea, Bell. Grab those two chairs and I'll go get our drinks."

The bar was nearly empty, with only two of the old miners left. The two that closed us in the mine and pulled rifles on us when we came out. I came up to the bar beside them. They looked at me, but their rummy eyes didn't seem to recognize me. They just turned back to their whiskey.

I ordered two glasses of that good Amador zin we had before and brought them into the lobby. Two others had sat down by Bell in recently vacated seats.

"Granny! Gwyn! It's wonderful to see you. How… when…"

"Set yourself down, dear. We've had quite a time."

"Uh… can I get you two anything to drink?"

"No thank you, Charles," Gwyn said. "We had so much tea on our trip here, we cannot drink anymore."

"Is Freesia here?" Bell asked.

"She is. However, she has been sleeping a lot since her ordeal at the cavern. Yana and I have been conferring about what to do to help her survive cat old age until we can figure out how to bring her back to her human form. Right now, sleeping is good for her."

"But how did you get here?" My turn to ask a question.

"Funny story," Granny began. "After you dropped me off at the yacht harbor, I boarded Gwyn's boat to visit with her. We were sitting in her galley sipping tea when we noticed the boat was rocking quite a bit. Gwyn thought it was because a large boat created waves as it went by in the harbor. Not so. Gwyn's boat had been untied from the dock and was heading out of the harbor mouth and into the bay."

"I saw that happen," I told Granny.

"What?" Granny and Gwyn said together.

"Well, with Grandfather's help. He added directions on how to envision family."

"Ah. Say, Gwyn, could you see Charles watching us?"

"No. I didn't. Spirit guides from other cultures are impossible to read for me."

"Where you able to see anything else, Charles dear?"

I told Granny how blurry everything became and how I needed to recharge my medicine bag and everything that went into it.

"So when you fixed your medicine bag, did you try to see us again?" Granny asked.

"I did. And I saw Dean. How did he get on your boat?"

"It was him, or rather his essence, who was moving the boat, through his magic. He finally appeared to us and said we must return to Volcano."

"Dean saw me. He looked straight at me and motioned with his mouth 'Volcano'. We left right away and came here only to find that Dean's house had been torched. We went to see, and the house is intact. Only the interior is burned. Very odd."

"Dean told us what had happened. Another assassin. Dean escaped and may be in the wizard world with his family."

"How did you get here?" Bell asked. "Did someone drive you?"

"Yes," Gwyn answered. "Dean made sure my boat ended up at a dock in Stockton. Reverend Stagnaro was there waiting for us. He was driving the Wheelers' black Mercedes. We got here right after you. Oh, and we're all checked into the same rooms we had before."

Granny added, "Yes, we are. Like Yogi Berra said, it's deja vu all over again."

"Who's Yogi Berra?" Bell asked.

Granny and Gwyn smiled at her. I would tell her later.

Chapter 22

It had been a long eventful day for all of us. We said our goodnights and went to our rooms.

The following morning Bell and I reluctantly rose at six. After showering and getting dressed, it was after seven when we walked into the restaurant for the breakfast buffet. It was already getting crowded with all the people who obviously came here for the holidays. Granny and Gwyn arrived earlier and commandeered a table.

We sat down and I sighed as I looked at the lovely Christmas tree in the corner.

Being Christmas Eve, the hotel chefs had put out a larger and more elaborate selection of breakfast items including a portable single burner propane stove where one of the chefs was making eggs anyway you wanted. There was even a whole ham another chef was slicing.

Having not eaten much the day before, Bell and I filled our plates with eggs Benedict, ham, and fruit salad. Granny and Gwyn, both not eating meat, got oatmeal and a container of yoghurt.

Between mouthfuls, I asked Granny, "So, where is Paul, the Reverend? Is he over at the Inn again?"

"No." Granny said after swallowing a spoonful of oatmeal. "He drove back to his church in Sutter Creek. He said he has to prepare for his Christmas Eve mass."

"I wonder what's going on in his Elm Street Mission in Santa Cruz. The Reverend usually has daily meals for the down and out there."

"He said he has a young deacon who is taking care of his church while he's in Sutter Creek. Both places will be serving turkeys for Christmas tomorrow."

"That's pretty cool," Bell said. "He seems to really want to help the unfortunate."

After eating our fill, we sat around a while longer drinking coffee. Granny and Gwyn drank herbal teas. I asked Granny, "Do you want to go up and check out Dean's house?"

"No. There is nothing more we can do about that."

"Yana is right," Gwyn said. "I was able to envision last night from the locals in the other room about some bright flash, like the one in Santa Cruz. The volunteer fire people here assumed it was a gas explosion. They all said it was a miracle Dean was not in the house at the time. Well, we know otherwise. Right, Yana?"

"We all do."

"So, Granny, what should we do today? I mean, Dean said to

come here. Why?"

"Because I want to take you to the Masonic cave."

"Dean!" All of us said at once. Like before, he seemed to appear out of nowhere. Granny and Gwyn took it in stride. Bell and I both started.

"We're so happy to see you," Granny said, saying what we all felt. "Gwyn and I were nervous about her boat moving on its own until you showed up. Or rather an image of you showed up. Impressive."

Dean smiled. At least his mouth smiled. His eyes looked sad. Or concerned. "Thank you, my good friends. I am sorry to have brought you all back here." His smile disappeared. "I always thought I could do everything on my own. I have done that for so long, but you all have been so helpful. I am humbled by your friendship. But, please, I could really use more of your help."

"Dean, we are here for you."

Dean continued. "Before I was attacked the night before last, I was using my wand to try to see how the assassins are getting dispatched. Someone, or something was able to tune into my wand's magical reception."

"Really?" I queried. "Your wand has a signal?"

"I am afraid so. It is a signal that originates in the wizard world. Someone tapped into it, and before I knew it, an assassin showed up. I was able to transport myself out just as the assassin's deathly light broke through my door and windows. Unfortunately, I could not see the face of the assassin. But because I live in the woods here, I use magic to make my house fireproof. Many of us in Volcano are afraid of wildfires through these hills. That is why only the interior of my house got burned."

"Any idea how these assassins are able to create that bright light?" Bell asked.

"No. I am afraid not. I am hoping with your help we can find out. I hope we can surprise them. Maybe stop the threat. But we do need to go to the Masonic cave. We must meet the others there."

"The others?" I asked.

"My nephew, Del, and his children, Marty and Dria. Tegan has been training them when she is able. But they are not quite ready to return yet. However, I am afraid the assassin now knows about the cave and its portal."

"Dean, the caves are not good for our kind," Granny warned. "I don't have my bag of protective items. It is still at Charles's home in Santa Cruz."

"Dear Yana," Dean said with a soothing voice. "That old wive's tale is no more than that."

"I am not an old wife," Granny complained, then gave a Mona Lisa type of smile. "Explain please."

"Okay. I will try do my best to explain. I think I might have mentioned this before, but some of these marble and limestone caves are portals to our world. In the past, we promoted those cave fears to your kind to keep you away. Over a hundred years ago, we were all very paranoid of witches and warlocks, mainly due to those who practiced the black arts and tried to use them against us. Little did we know that one of our kind, a sorceress, who also secretly practiced the black arts would be our undoing. Her attempt to weaken us so she could be leader backfired and killed everyone, and I am sure, included her. Up until then we had to keep our world secret. No more. No more. It is only my family left. No reason to keep it secret from you, my friends, anymore. I am hoping with all of us on the other side of the portal, we can surprise the assassin. I hope to capture him and interrogate him to find who the dispatcher is."

"Maybe between Bell, Granny, and me, we can lure the assassin in and set an immediate binding spell so you can question him."

Granny frowned. "Charles, dear, I don't want to be an old stick in the mud, but we are yet to find out the assassin's real powers and if they can be bound. Like what happened to that black sorceress, it could backfire on us."

"There may be another way," Dean said. "We know that these assassins seem mortal, as we know from the death of the two who were hanging out with the Wheelers. What we don't know is how they create that deadly light, but it does seem to be their only ability. They do not seem to use any device, so it is possible it comes from their eyes. If we can cover the assassin, hopefully they cannot use it."

Some more people came in for breakfast and stood at the door waiting for a table to open up. We were finished and just talking, so Bell suggested we go outside, sit at a picnic table, and finish planning our day with Dean.

It was chilly and cloudy. The hotel desk had a weather forecast pinned to a small bulletin board, and it said there was a chance of snow. A white Christmas, I thought.

Bell, Granny, Gwyn, and I excused ourselves to Dean and went to our rooms to put on warmer jackets. Bell and Granny both had long, red down jackets, Gwyn had put on a sweatshirt that didn't look warm enough, but said it was toasty. I wore my shearling-lined jean jacket.

When we returned to Dean, he had started a fire in the fire pit next to the picnic tables. A few flakes of snow were drifting around.

Dean spoke. "We had better make our plans quickly before the snowing gets serious."

Chapter 23

For the next hour we discussed different scenarios about how to subdue the assassin. However, the more Dean thought about it, the more he didn't want to have the assassin finding how to get into the wizard's world, an ancient land within our own. A different time and place.

"What if he only follows us into the cave but prevent him from breaking through the portal?" I suggested. "Dean, you and Granny should go in. Can you seal the portal after you go in?"

"It is always sealed. My wand opens and closes it. There is another way to open the portal, but until my family can return to this world safely, I need to keep that secret for now. Not just to you, but to anyone with abilities who might be able to tune into your thoughts. We don't know who the assassin's dispatcher is or where he or she is located. Or, if the dispatcher is magical in some way."

"What can I do?" Gwyn asked. "I cannot read the assassin's mind or know where or when he could be. Unless…"

"Unless?" Granny asked.

"Unless I can give Freesia energy enough to spy for us and let us know where the assassin is and when he arrives. We know Dean's wand seems to send a signal the assassin seems to pick up on now. Freesia can keep a lookout. She and I can keep in touch telepathically. I just need to rouse her."

"Let me help," Dean said. "I cannot hear her, but I can use my power to make her feel younger. It is temporary, but should last a day or two. Gwyn, can you wake her and ask her permission for me to do that? If she is willing to help, that is."

"I will try. She is awfully weak. We need to remove her curse as soon as possible. She is nearing the end of a cat's lifespan. Yes. I will try."

Gwyn woke a very sleepy Freesia and told her what Dean could do to help her so she could help us. Gwyn also told her that once we know who the dispatcher is and is stopped for good, it would be safe for all of us to attempt breaking her curse. Freesia agreed.

Gwyn motioned for Dean to come into her room. Freesia looked up at him with half closed eyes. She could barely sit up. Dean didn't wave his wand for fear of alerting the assassin. Instead, he put his hand over Freesia's head, closed his eyes, and a spark seemed to jump from his hand to Freesia. Her eyes went wide, and she let out a loud meow as she jumped up on all fours, did a cat-like stretch, then sat down on her hind quarters.

"Madam Seren. Please thank Mister Prentiss for his magic. I feel

much younger and energetic now and ready to help."

"Ah, my lovely Freesia. I am hoping this will be over quickly so my friends can attempt to reverse your curse." Gwyn had tears in her eyes.

"Please do not cry, Madam Seren. If they cannot help me, no matter. It has been an honor to work with you. Now. Let us all head for the cave."

The weather was changing for the worse. A cold rain interspersed with snowflakes was falling. We had all gone into the lobby, as had many of the other guests, to keep warm by the fire.

"It's too yucky outside to walk to the caves," I said. "I'll go get my van. I'll drive us there."

Any other time we would have walked the half mile to the Masonic caves, but not this time. We piled into the van. Freesia jumped in and sat next to Gwyn, who put her arm around Freesia and held her close.

The drive to the caves was short, but I kept the van slow in case there was ice on the road. The rain had now turned to snow and was steadily falling. I pulled into a small parking area by a couple of picnic tables already getting a thin dusting of snow.

"Okay," Dean said. "Up that path is the cave where the gold rush era Masons had several of their first meetings. The portal is in there. Gwyn, please tell Freesia to stay out of sight behind a rock just inside the entrance. She will be safe there and out of the weather. She can warn you when the assassin arrives. I am sure as soon as I use my wand to open the portal, the assassin will tune into it and arrive almost immediately."

"We better get up there right away," Bell said. It's getting colder and that path is wet and could freeze over soon."

"Charles, can you carry Freesia?" Gwyn asked. "She is a little too heavy for me."

"Be glad to."

Freesia jumped over the seat and got in my lap.

"Thank you, Mister Blue. I will do my best to help and keep you informed if anyone shows up."

We got out of the van and began walking up the path.

"Uh... Charles, the sign says look out for rattlesnakes." Bell pointed out.

"I don't think we'll have to worry. Snakes are cold blooded. They'd only come out on warm days."

A minute later we reached the cave entrance. I sat Freesia down and she padded over and hid behind a rock. The cave was so dark that even Freesia's white fur was hard to see where she was hiding. She looked like a small pile of snow.

"Okay," Dean said. Are you all ready? Fingers crossed we can capture this character. Hopefully, we won't have to kill him."

Granny was saying something in Romani I had never heard before. I suddenly felt like something enveloped me and I shivered. I noticed Bell and Gwyn shivered too. "What did you just do, Granny? I've never heard you say that incantation before."

"I wanted to make sure I could do an incantation in a cave. It worked. Dean was right. Anyway, I can only tell you it is a type of protection spell. A force field around the cave and all of us in here. The assassin will bump into it and maybe use his white flash to burn through it. As soon as he uses it, we can pounce and subdue him. I hope. Like Dean said, fingers crossed. Dean?"

"Let's go then."

Dean's wand lit up and what was just a rock wall became a beautiful scene of green fields, pine and oak trees, and sunlight.

"Ladies? Charles? Follow me."

We did and walked into a comfortably warm environment. I looked back and saw snow falling outside the cave entrance.

"Incredible!" I exclaimed. "This looks a lot like the countryside around Volcano."

"It is, but of a different age. Think medieval times. You might even find Reverend Stagnaro's Miwok ancestors somewhere around here." Dean looked around and sighed. "I have not been here for a long, long time."

"A car approaches. It is pulling in right behind Mister Blue's van."

"Dean." Granny tapped him on his shoulder. "Freesia just told us a car is out there."

I noticed Gwyn looked worried. "Gwyn. What's wrong?"

"Freesia told me she came out of hiding and was watching down below. I just told her to get out of sight, but I am afraid she was noticed. I feel it."

"Look. There's Freesia."

She ran in through the portal and behind Gwyn. She was gazing at the cave's entrance.

"Freesia. What's wrong?" Bell asked telepathically.

"I know who it is who drove up. I came out of hiding to say hello and saw evil instead of love."

"Who was it?"

"Reverend Stagnaro."

Chapter 24

"Stagnaro!" said the four of us at once. Those of us who could understand Freesia. Dean heard us and repeated the exclamation.

"Why?" Bell asked. "What changed in him? He exuded such good will and charm. I mean he helped Tegan save Marty."

"We need to capture him and find out why he's turned on us," I said. "We should not try to kill him… unless…"

"Unless?" Dean queried.

"Unless there is no other option."

"There is always another option." This voice was only inside my head.

"Grandfather?"

Everyone looked at me like I was nuts. Then Bell and Granny realized why I said that and nodded.

"You are present in a time of great understanding of shamanism,

magic, and sorcery. Your recharged medicine bag has much more power where you now stand. Use it. You know what to do, my dear Grandson."

"Holy cow! Everyone hide somewhere to get away from the white light! I know what to do!"

"Are you sure?" Dean asked. "Maybe all of us…"

"No. Go. Please. Everybody. My grandfather's guiding me."

Bell and Granny knew what I meant and pulled Gwyn and Dean away to hide behind some trees. Freesia ran to follow Gwyn.

The timing was perfect. As soon as they were hidden, Paul, the Reverend Stagnaro, still in his black outfit and clerical collar, stood in front of the cave entrance staring at me. He started to enter and was knocked back a step as he hit Granny's force field. I could see him getting very angry and his eyes were bright red like he was possessed. Except now that bright red was turning white, and I could see him preparing to blast through the barrier at me.

I held onto my medicine bag, stared straight back at the Reverend, and recited a quick Ohlone incantation.

The blinding white light shot out of his eyes and broke through the barrier. I was expecting some kind of jolt or intense heat, but nothing happened. His light hit close in front of me then bounced back through the portal, hitting the Reverend and reentering his eyes. He fell back to the cave entrance and collapsed on the path. The now heavy falling snow was accumulating on his unconscious body.

I yelled for the others to come out of hiding as I ran to the Reverend's side and checked his pulse. It was weak, but there. Just in case, I put a binding spell on him. I didn't know if it would work with one who had abilities like he had, but Granny and Bell ran up and did the same. Dean touched his wand to both the Reverend's hands. They seemed to lock together behind his back as if they had invisible handcuffs.

Gwyn and Freesia were the last to come back through the portal and to the cave entrance.

What happened next would be very hard to explain when Bell wrote about it in her journals.

Freesia approached the unconscious Reverend, sniffed at him and did that cat thing of rubbing her cheek up against his face, then she laid down on his chest.

And began morphing. Morphing into a beautiful seventeen-year-old girl with long pure white hair. Unfortunately, naked.

Gwyn acted fast and took her long coat off and put it around Freesia. Gwyn, Granny, and Bell led her through the portal into the warmth of the wizard world. Dean and I both stood there in the cold with our mouths open, then realized we were shivering and followed them through the portal, carrying the Reverend with us. Dean turned around and closed the portal.

"Bell. What just happened?" I asked her.

"I have no idea. I assumed we would break her spell. Could Freesia have had a connection to the Reverend some time ago? Oh. Look. She seems to be in shock. After twenty years as a cat…"

"If she was seventeen when the Ramahi witch bitch cursed her, you would think she would be… what? In her late thirties? Forties? Older? Do you think she will sleep and age like… well, like you did?"

Bell didn't like that memory but has learned to accept it now that we were permanently together. *I hope.* Bell sighed. "Maybe.

Maybe not. She wasn't asleep all that time. She was alive. Perhaps she reverted back to herself at the time of her curse."

"That would be nice for her, having a full life ahead. Granny? Gwyn? Let me use my medicine bag to ease Freesia's mind."

"Yes, dear Charles," Granny said. "Hurry. She needs to breathe easy before she hyperventilates. The change took a lot out of her."

I went over to Freesia and sat down beside her. I reached out to hold her hand and she quickly pulled it away. Her eyes were wide with panic. I recited a short Ohlone spell to calm her enough for me to recite the full healing spell. The panic left her eyes and she looked at me. I heard her speak to me telepathically, but very weakly.

"*You... I recognize you. Nice man. Am I... Can I...*" She started speaking out loud but seemed to have trouble forming words.

This time she reached out and took my right hand. Holding my medicine bag with my other hand I recited the full healing spell. She smiled at me then looked up at Gwyn who sat down on Freesia's other side and touched her face. Gwyn had tears in her eyes.

"Are you okay, dear Gwyn?" Granny asked.

"Tears of joy my dear Yana. Tears of joy."

"Dean! Charles! The Reverend is waking up," Granny noticed.

"He is bound and is no threat to us in this world," Dean said.

Reverend Stagnaro groaned and tried to raise his hand to rub his face but couldn't with both hands bound behind him. He then looked up at Dean then looked around at the rest of us. His eyes kept closing and opening as he moved his head back and forth.

"Ow. My head is splitting. What happened? Why can't I move my arms? Uh... where am I? How did I get here?"

The Reverend's eyes were not red anymore and looked normal, except for being very bloodshot.

Dean answered. "Paul. Do you know what just happened? That you attacked us?"

"Attacked? Why? Why would I do that? I was helping prepare food at my mission in Sutter Creek. How did I get here?" Suddenly, his eyes closed.

"Gwyn?" I looked at her and could see she was in a trance. "Gwyn? Are you…"

"*Shush, Charles,*" Granny told me telepathically. "*Gwyn is getting into the Reverend's mind. She can while he is weak.*"

We all kept quiet for another minute until we noticed that Freesia got up and came over and put her hand on Gwyn's shoulder. Gwyn came out of her trance, smiled, and put her hand over Freesia's.

"Now I can see why Freesia's curse was lifted," Gwyn said. "Reverend Paul Stagnaro's half-sister was that black witch Jean Stagnaro, later Jean Ramahi, Pete's mother, who put the curse on Freesia. It turns out that only a Stagnaro family member could reverse the curse. Freesia, as a cat, was able to pick up a particular scent that let her know the Reverend was of that same family. She rubbed her own scent on the Reverend's face which started her change back to human form."

"That is wonderful, Gwyn. "Bell said with tears in her eyes.

"Yes, so wonderful. But did you find out why Paul attacked us?" Granny asked.

"That I could not find out. Something blocked me. Not him." Gwyn pointed at the reawakening Reverend. "Paul is clean now. Dean? You can release him. He is back to his old self." Dean did and reached down to help Paul up to his feet.

Granny spoke up. "Dean. Can you reopen the portal? We should get back to the hotel where it's warm."

"Freesia," Bell said. "I have some extra clothes in my bag you can put on. Uh…Freesia, are you okay?"

She was looking around trying to take everything in standing up as a human. For twenty years she saw the world very close to the ground. "I am okay. Oh. So… It is strange to be able to… to talk out loud. Madam Seren. Thank you for saving my life. I am so… so much in your debt. I will be out of your way soon."

"Freesia, dear. You do not have to leave. You have kept me company for so many years, you became part of me. You are family. I… I would be so lonely without you. I would love you to stay."

Tears were forming in both Freesia's and Gwyn's eyes.

Dean opened the portal.

Chapter 25

While we had been in the wizard world, outside, in our world, it had stopped snowing. There were several inches of snow on the path going down to the parking area and on top of the van. The Reverend had driven up in the Wheelers' black Mercedes, but not feeling up to driving yet, he left it there to pick up when he felt better. He got in the van with the rest of us.

The van was cold when we got in, but the heater worked well as soon as the engine warmed up.

The road back to the hotel was slick, so I drove slow and careful. When I pulled into the parking area in front of the hotel and put on the brakes, the wheels locked, and the van slowly slid up to the sidewalk and came to an abrupt stop.

"Whew. I should see about getting some chains for this van. I'll ask at the front desk if there are any around here I can purchase.

We'll probably need them to drive out of here when we head home."

Granny said, "Let's go to our rooms. Paul, come with me. We have a lot to talk about."

Granny and Gwyn led the Reverend through the lobby and out the back toward their rooms in the annex. Bell and I followed with Freesia and went to our room to freshen up. The three of us were very thirsty, and each of us drank two glasses of water. Refreshed, Bell gave some of her clothes to Freesia. Fortunately, their feet were about the same size, so Bell gave her some socks and her extra pair of shoes. Her sneakers.

It was after one in the afternoon, and we were getting hungry for lunch. Dean said he would be in the bar to wait for us so we could eat together.

When Bell, Freesia, and I returned, the restaurant room was full, but Dean had commandeered a table and several chairs in the bar area. Bell and Freesia sat down. I went to the front desk to ask about chains. I came back a couple of minutes later and sat down.

"No chains in town, but the lady at the desk said she'd call a tow service from Sutter Creek to bring and install the chains."

"Should we wait for Yana and Gwyn before we order?" Dean asked.

"I don't know how long they'll be talking to the Reverend." I answered. "I'm sure they're trying to find out what caused him to become possessed."

"Let's go ahead and order," Bell said. "I'm starved."

Freesia was looking around with curiosity.

"Freesia. This must seem so different being inside here now,"

Bell said. "Are you okay?"

Freesia reached across the table and held Bell's hand. "Yes. I'm fine. Just a little disoriented. I feel like I haven't eaten real food for ages. Can I have a hamburger?"

Dean, Bell, and I ordered the same, grilled ham and cheese sandwiches. The ham was fresh baked and sliced thicker than usual. It smelled and tasted like the ham my mother used to make at Christmas time when I was in grade school. She would bake a whole ham with cloves stuck into the outside, then remove them to slice it. I would suck the ham's juice off of the used clove pieces. *Sigh*. The cheese was good sharp cheddar. Freesia did get a hamburger but was only able to eat barely half of it. She felt it would take a while to get used to eating as a real human instead of a cat. Or, as she said telepathically to me, as a real witch. We finished our food and were ordering coffee when Granny and Gwyn came in.

"Where's the Reverend?" I asked Granny.

"We walked him back to the Inn where he had stayed before. He checked in and we went to his room to talk some more. He's pretty worn out from his possession, so we left him there to sleep. I put a heavy-duty protection spell on his room... just in case someone tries to enter to possess him again."

"So, it was a possession," I commented. "Do you think the other assassins were also possessed? Those two that died who were chasing us..."

"If they were weakened warlocks or witches, or some kind of shaman, they could have been easily possessed like Paul was. If they were, I wish we knew sooner. We might have been able to save them like we did Paul, now that we know how to turn the white light flame back onto them to break the possession."

"Does that mean that there is no one hiring assassins but rather taking possession of our kind to make them assassins? Weaker ones?" Bell asked.

"Something about this makes me wonder…" I stopped talking when our coffee came. The waitress brought a French press coffee maker and was pushing the wire screen plunger down then poured out four demi cups. Freesia pushed hers away telling us it may take a while for her to get used to coffee again. The waitress then asked Granny and Gwyn if they wanted anything. They both ordered plain yoghurt and herbal tea. The waitress left.

"You were saying dear Charles?"

"I started thinking that there's something familiar about the white light and fires. This strong power and possession is similar to what Pete Ramahi and his mother could do. However, it's without the witch or warlock ashes. We know that Pete's family is gone, but could there be another Ramahi, or Ramahi follower out there that the Wheelers contracted?"

"I don't think so, but it is something we should check out. I doubt we can do anything here for now, unless… Yes Dean?"

"Tegan might be able to help."

I looked at Dean quizzically. "You know I expected to see Tegan and Del and his kids when we went through your portal."

"Remember, Charles, Tegan currently cannot come out in the daytime. Even in the wizard world. I hope one of these days she can be out anytime and anywhere. She and her family are in hiding not far from where we were. She is training the others in there."

"But how can she help?" Bell asked.

"The nights are long this time of year. She intends to spend more time training them and to locate where the possessions are emanating from. She and I will work together after sunset. Whoever is causing this has to be close for it to have affected the Reverend so quickly."

"Granny, are any of us at risk of possession?" I asked.

"No. No, dear. What Gwyn and I deduced from talking to Paul, he has only a shaman's power and we feel he is susceptible. Remember when young Marty was snatched from certain death in his VW van, Paul acted as a conduit for Tegan to save Marty. Other than minor healing spells he does at his missions, his only real power is as a conduit for others, like Tegan. Maybe for us too. Relax, my dear grandson. We're safe."

"Maybe being a conduit was what got him possessed. Maybe someone or something got through to him that way. Maybe the others were similar to Paul. Oh. By the way. Was the Reverend able to tell you how he got possessed?"

"No. The poor man can't remember a thing. Not how it happened, or while it was happening. I used a hypnotic spell on him, but even that didn't work. His mind is blank for those hours as if he was in a coma. Someone or something took control of him without his knowing it."

"Granny, he was really lucky that when we turned the light back on him, it didn't kill him. Instead, it sure knocked the possessor out of his head."

"Yes, but where did it come from? Where did it go?"

Chapter 26

It was after 2:30 when we finished our coffees and teas. All of us, except Dean, felt very tired from the trip into the wizard world. Dean told us it had to do with the time distance. Stepping through the portal slipped us back two millennium. Same world, different time. Wizards are not affected, but other people, with abilities or not, become very thirsty and tire easily.

Even though it was only midafternoon, Bell and I went back to our room, laid down and fell asleep fully clothed. Granny went to her room and did the same. Freesia went with Gwyn and the two of them also fell asleep. Gwyn in her bed, Freesia, now human, still curled up cat-like, in the easy chair. It may take her a while to get used to a bed.

Dean went back up the hill to his house. He told us he planned to do a little wizard-style magic to cleanup his burned-out home so he could move back in right away.

When Bell and I finally woke up, refreshed, the sun had already set. We realized we had been asleep for over three hours. We also realized we were not alone.

"Good evening Mister Blue and Miss Beltane."

"Hi Charles. Good to see you and Bell again. Happy Christmas Eve."

"Tegan! Del!" Bell and I both said at the same time. We jumped out of bed, and I vigorously shook his hand. Bell gave him a big hug.

Bell said before I could, "Del. It is so good to see that you're okay. We were so worried when you and your daughter first disappeared. Tegan explained it to us. And finding Marty must have been a relief for you."

"It was. When I thought Marty was dead, I cried. When I found him, I cried again, but with happiness. It still puts a lump in my throat thinking about it."

"Ah. Bell, look there." I pointed to a stick protruding from Del's jeans right front pocket. Del looked down at what I was pointing at and chuckled.

"We stopped to see Uncle Dean first. He gave me my own wand. Dria and Marty are at Dean's getting theirs. We'll be going back to our world… still such an odd thing for me to say…" Del smiled. "We will practice with them. Mom has been wonderful teaching us."

"Del, will you and Marty come back to Santa Cruz to play in your band again?"

"We will. It is a fun way to earn money when we're back in the real world again. Our two albums sold well. The second even went platinum."

"Platinum?" Bell asked.

"It sold over a million copies."

"I am so proud of my boy," Tegan said as she kissed his cheek. Del's faced turned red with embarrassment. "Dear, you have come so far since playing in that terrible band with that evil Ramahi fellow."

"Thanks Mom. We should get back to Uncle Dean's so I can grab my kids and get back to our world."

"I am going to stay here as long as it is dark and try to find out who this possessor is."

"Can we help?" Bell asked Tegan.

"I am not sure you should. Are not you afraid of being possessed?"

"It's impossible. Charles and I are too powerful. And Charles has a double whammy."

"Say what?" Del asked.

I answered. "Besides inheriting my warlock abilities from my grandmother's Roma side, I inherited Indian shamanism from my grandfather's Ohlone side. I can create very potent protection spells that can help reverse any white flames being projected at us. With Bell's and Granny's protection abilities added to it, we're pretty formidable."

Granny knocked on the door. Bell let her in. She immediately hugged Del.

"So good to see you. We were worried. Hello Tegan. It has been…"

"Ah, you must be Yana," Tegan cut in quickly. "So good to meet you."

I noticed a little haughty exchange between the two. I'm sure Bell did too. *Did they know each other before?*

I think Del might have noticed too. He went back to what we had been discussing. "What about Gwyn?"

"That's doubtful," Granny answered. "Gwyn is not a witch. She is a seer. A prophetess. A fortune teller. Well, for humans mostly. Not for our kind."

"Granny, I'm sorry to say that's not really true. When Bell and I first visited Gwyn, she was able to read our pasts."

"Ah. But dear Charles, she cannot foretell our futures. That is what I was referring to. Our pasts are a different thing. She can see what occurred in our pasts quite well." Granny chuckled. "Not mine, though. I can block her."

I shrugged and got back to the issues at hand. "Del, what about you and your kids? You're all still in training. Is it possible for any of you to get possessed?"

Tegan answered. "Wizards are not susceptible. Even when Del and my grandchildren had no idea they were wizards, they could not get possessed. It is different for weak or weakened witches and warlocks."

"Mother." Del spoke up. "I should go get Marty and Dria and head back to our world. Please be careful here." Del held his mother's hand, raised it up and kissed it. Tegan put her other hand up to his face.

"I will be fine. I am a survivor, my dear son."

Del pulled his new wand out. "Well, this is still alien to me, but here goes." His wand glowed on the end and Del disappeared right in front of us, just like Tegan did the first time she visited Bell and me.

"Now... my friends, I must also go. I know you want to help, and I will come back for you after I look around the area. Bell, Charles, you will know I am around by the glowing of your rings. Goodbye for now."

Tegan had also been given a new wand by Dean. She pulled it out and it glowed, as did our rings, and she also disappeared.

"Did you feel that?" Bell asked me. "When Del and Tegan left, I felt a little shock each time. I felt like I could have followed them."

We left our room and walked into the lobby where the others sat in front of the fire. On the way, Granny explained, "Your rings. When you both got them and they started glowing, I thought they would alert you to danger. Now, I'm not sure what all they can do. They glowed when Tegan or Del were invisibly crossing realms, and they glowed just now when they both left. I am not sure why the slight shocks occur. Bell, I remember you were, what, sixteen when you made those rings?"

"Yes. However, I didn't add the amber pieces."

"Ah. Your mother, Constance, added those, Bell. I've barely started reading your mother's journals and must read more of them when we go home and see if she explains the glowing. Are they with you in Santa Cruz?"

"No Yana. I hid them in the Victorian in San Francisco. And, no, those working on the house will not find them. I can get them for you when Charles and I move back to the city."

"Gwyn, your boat is still in the Stockton harbor. How will you get it back to Santa Cruz?" Granny asked.

Gwyn slyly smiled and laughed. "Dear Yana. I do not just live on my boat. I sometimes take it out to do a little fishing for my and Freesia's dinner. That is something I really enjoy. So, I can pilot my boat back. I will have to get some fuel first, but the three of us can head back when we finish this. Charles can drop us off close to the pier before that lovely pair head home."

Gwyn's smile disappeared as she looked at the back door.

"What's wrong?" Granny asked.

"Look there."

Just outside the door, out of sight of the other hotel visitors sitting by the fire, was Dean. He had a look of panic on his face. He motioned at us to come outside. We got out of our seats, which filled up with other visitors as soon as we stood up.

"Dean, dear. What's wrong? Granny asked.

"What I thought was impossible, happened. Another assassin somehow followed Del and has entered the wizard world."

Chapter 27

"No!" Granny said. "You said that it was impossible. Oh, my gods and goddesses Dean. Who is possessed this time? Another shaman or a warlock or witch? Are Del and his children in jeopardy? What about Tegan? How did someone or something follow him into your world?"

"That is what I am worried about. This new assassin must have tuned into Del's wand when he went to pick up his kids then again when they went to the wizard world. Hopefully, they are hiding. But I doubt the assassin knows about Tegan's power, so I am hoping she can surprise it when she returns. And I have no idea who the assassin is this time or who controls him… or her. I am heading there now. For as long as I have lived, I have been on my own and able to take care of myself. These assassin possessions are so different than anything I have seen before, and

I cannot put my finger on it. I am embarrassed to ask, but can I count on you to help again?"

"Of course." Bell and I answered together, even though we had no idea what to expect or what to do. I added, "That's why we're here. Hopefully, I can do the same to this new assassin that I did to the Reverend." Granny said she would help too.

Gwyn said she wanted to stay back with Freesia, who was still weak and needs to get used to being a witch again. Gwyn's type of ability would not be of much help this time.

"I must quickly return to my home to gather a few items for our trip back to the Masonic cave. Normally, I would just wave my wand for me to go to my world, but I cannot do that for your kind. We must all go through the portal together again."

"What are you retrieving from your place?" I asked.

"A couple of artifacts. You will see."

With that, he waved his wand and disappeared.

"Bell, notice this." I held up my ring. "When Dean disappears, our rings don't glow."

"Odd. Mine too."

As usual, Granny had an answer. "He's just journeying in our own time back to his home. I am sure your rings would glow if he disappeared to his wizard world."

"I guess that's logical," I said. "Well, logical if I'll ever understand time traveling to and from the wizard world."

When we were napping it had snowed again. As we headed for the van, it started snowing heavier. The last snow melted already and now over an inch was on the road. Fortunately, just then the tow service arrived and installed chains on the rear tires of my van. After Bell paid the man, she and I got in the front bucket seats and Granny and Dean slid onto the back seat.

With the chains on, I couldn't drive over twenty-five. The half mile took nearly fifteen minutes to travel. I parked as close to the path as I could. No other cars were there.

"Okay you three," Dean said. "Take these and put them in your pockets."

"Marbles?" I questioned.

"No. No. Look close. These artifacts are ancient lava globules from my world. See the runes carved in them? These were made by your kind who coexisted, albeit not in a friendly way, with my kind more than a thousand years before I was born. If necessary, you…"

Granny cut in. "…throw it at an assailant. Yes, Dean. I know what these are. I've seen them before a long, long time ago. They are like mini hand grenades. They are dangerous…"

"Ah. You know. I was just about to say that Yana. Bell, Charles, be at least ten feet away from whoever you throw these at. Any closer and you might be affected by the concussion. Also, once thrown, they can be picked up and used again… and again."

"Granny, you've never told me about these lava things before."

"I didn't tell you, because I've been suppressing the memory of a sad and bad time in our history. Someday I will tell you. But not now. We have a job to do here."

"Let me go into my world first," Dean suggested. "I will make sure the portal is clear, then I will come back for you."

Dean pulled out his wand, waved it, and disappeared from where he was sitting next to Granny. This time, our rings glowed, and we felt a slight shock. Granny, having been next to Dean, also got a shock.

"Oh my gods and goddesses." Granny caught her breath. "I'll never get used to that."

"Granny. Sometimes when our rings glow, and we get the shock, we feel we could travel with Tegan or Dean. It's a really odd feeling. Like a pull…"

"I really need to read all of Constance's journals. She must have something in them about your rings. There must be some kind of magic… maybe there's even wizard type magic in those rings."

"Yana," Bell said. "My mother never mentioned anything to me about our family background. Did she ever say anything to you?"

"No, Bell, she didn't. She was a very dear friend I met a very long time ago when we were in high school in San Francisco. We knew we were both special and bonded right away. But she never told me where she came from then or where she went after graduation. I didn't see her again until she came into my fortune telling business at Playland, telling me she wanted to open a magic store that became the Mystic Eye Occult Shop. Bell, she was a dear, sweet woman. Ah… I'm feeling a shock again."

"Uh… Granny. Our rings are glowing again. Dean must be… ouch!"

Dean reappeared next to Granny.

"The entrance is all clear. We can go now. Why are you looking at me like that?"

I answered. "You're traveling to and from your place and time shocks us. And our rings make us feel like we could follow you. Very strange feeling."

"Hmm. I will have to look into that someday. Sorry for making you uncomfortable Yana. But… we must hurry. Let us go."

We got out of the van and followed Dean up the path to the cave entrance. We went inside and Dean opened the portal. We all went in, and he closed the portal behind us. It had also snowed in Dean's world, but not as much. A dusting of snow was crunching under our feet.

"Where do we go from here?" Bell asked Dean.

"Black Chasm Cavern. Yes, Bell, the natural entrance is a mile away. The walk is along an Indian trail that does not exist anymore in your time."

"Are there Indians around here now?" I asked.

"No. This time of year they are in the lower elevations, the area you call the Central Valley. The Miwok are hunters and gatherers and move to where game and fish are plentiful. The women gather acorns to grind for flat bread. Now. Enough of that. Follow me. Uh… Yana, will you be okay?"

"As usual, Charles can use his grandfather's medicine bag to keep me going. Yes. Let's go."

The winding trail took us forty-five minutes to reach the cavern's entrance. Granny tired out within five minutes, and I had to hold her hand to keep her walking easier. When we arrived, Bell and I were both winded and breathing hard. Dean, being as old or older than Granny didn't even break a sweat.

"You all catch your breath a few minutes before we go in. Remember, this is several thousand years before your time. There are no steps or guard rails in this cave. Follow me and step where I step."

We followed Dean closely. He took out his wand and lit our way once we got into the darkness of the interior. We must have walked a hundred yards or more when we heard voices. Dean turned to us and motioned for us to stop and be quiet. He turned his lit wand off. We could see a dim flickering light just ahead coming from a small side cave opening. We could also smell wood smoke.

Dean went on ahead while we waited hardly breathing. He looked into the side cave just as a bright flash knocked him down and blinded us.

Chapter 28

It took more than a minute for our eyes to readjust from the flash. I felt someone run by me. I was worried that while we were blinded, we were too susceptible to attack. I'm sure Bell and Granny felt the same way. Rubbing our eyes, Bell and I ran over to Dean who was conscious but still laying prone on the cave floor.

"Dean! Dean!" I nearly yelled, my voice echoing through the cavern. "Are you okay?"

"Uh. That was a surprise. Glad I had my wand up to protect me, or I might not be here now."

"Did you see who that was?" Bell asked.

"No. The flash came too quickly. I did hear whoever it was running away… toward you three. You did not see who it was? No. You were blinded too." Dean shakily stood up, nearly falling again. I grabbed my medicine bag and quickly recited an Ohlone healing spell. Dean let out a big sigh. "Ah. Much better. Thank you, Mister Blue. Now... Let us find my family. I am very worried. Watch your heads in here. This small cave opens into a very large and spectacular room that the Indians have used for hundreds of years." Dean turned on his wand again.

Even short Granny had to bend down a little to get through the connecting tunnel. The rest of us had to really bend over. Fortunately, the connector was only six feet long and opened into a large room. Dean said it was spectacular, but what I saw really took my breath away. Ribbons of delicate pure white stalactites hung like thousands of soda straws across the ceiling. Several huge columns looked like giant ice cream sundaes. Other stalactites of alternating colors were dripping onto matching stalagmites. Toward the back of the room a milky-white liquid was flowing from a hose-like stalactite into an equally white overflowing pool in a large, raised basin. The overflow disappeared down a very small shaft and I could hear its echoing splash twenty or thirty feet below. A section of floor looked like it had been dug and flattened. A fire pit was in the center. The fire was out, but there was still a glow from the embers.

"Holy sh... uh... holy cow!" I exclaimed. "Indians lived in here?"

"Well, your exclamation was partially right. This is a <u>holy</u> place for the Miwok. Ceremonies take place here in the late Spring through early Fall when the Indians are back in this area. This cavern is used by the Miwok shamans. Ritual training of the young takes place here. This is not a permanent living space for the Indians."

"So, who was here burning wood?" Bell asked. "Del? Tegan?"

"No. I think the fire was keeping whoever surprised us warm. I expected Tegan and Del and his kids to be in here waiting for us. They must have transported themselves to safety when this other person showed up. It must not be an assassin, or it would have finished us off while we were blinded. Maybe it is the possessor. Maybe not. I cannot tell. You?"

Bell had been thinking. "Well, whoever it was, when they ran by me, the sound of their feet was not heavy. Also, I caught a whiff of a familiar fragrance. I'm pretty sure it was a woman. Shorter than me. And she was not possessed. She was too determined to escape us. Not attack us."

"Let us leave this place and head back to the portal. Oh, and hold onto my artifacts, those lava globules, just in case. However, try not to use them indoors unless it is absolutely necessary."

An hour later we were back in our rooms at the hotel… minus Dean. He left to go back to his house to clean up the fire damage more. We barely sat down on the bed to relax when our rings started glowing again.

"Bell, sometimes our rings just glow on their own, and we don't feel any shock like when one of the wizards travels to their world. We need to find out more about our rings. Every time they glow, I really feel like we can travel like Dean does. Like we could follow him through time. I know Granny wants to know more about our rings too, but when we get back to our home in San Francisco, we should read your mother's journals before Granny does. She has so many secrets about her past, and it appears your mother did too. Yes, maybe we should have our own secrets now.

Let's read the journals then hide them. Or…"

"Create fake journals? Yana has been so good to both of us. Should we? I would feel so guilty. But…"

"But… Well, let's think about it. For now, I'm hungry and thirsty, and tired from that trip back in time with Dean. I don't want to sleep yet. Let's go to the bar and get some food… and drink. Maybe, they have some Christmas-type food left."

"I'm so sorry we couldn't be home in Santa Cruz so we could have a comfortable first Christmas together like you wanted. Maybe we could have a belated Christmas, or a New Year's celebration when we get home."

"Being with you anywhere is always Christmas for me. I love you, Bell."

"Ah. You're sweet. I love you too. I know it's late, but let's go eat and maybe get drunk on spiked eggnog or something. Then…" Bell looked at me with her bedroom eyes. "…you can unwrap your Christmas present."

"A present?"

"Yes. Me."

When we walked into the bar, all the tables in the bar and restaurant were full. Again, the five old-time miners were leaning on the counter throwing back shots of whiskey. Two seats were vacant right next to them. We sat down.

"Howdy shtrangersh… new in town?" Said the guy next to me, slurring his words and slightly spraying me with his slobbery whiskey breath. I picked up a napkin and wiped my face. If he was sober, he'd probably remember me.

"Nah," I replied, faking a backwoods drawl. "Been here fer a coon's age, Ernie." Bell kicked me under the counter. I smiled at her.

"Er... say, feller, how'd ya know ma name?" He might have been drunk, but when he took a good look at me, his eyes narrowed. "Ah. You been in..."

"This bar quite often," I shot back. "Heard your name mentioned. Tom, next to you too. Remember? You've seen us in here several times."

Ernie blinked. He was trying to remember. "Well, you both do seem familiar. Maybe... oh. You all needs drinks. Hey! Jerry! Give thish young couple thur poison."

Jerry, the bearded bartender, came over and took our drink order. I asked for a menu, and he told us the dining room was closing shortly. He said we could still order food at the bar. He reached under the counter and plopped a menu in front of us. A minute later he sat my beer and Bell's wine on the counter along with two glasses of water.

Ernie and his mining buddy Tom got up and left, stumbling out the bar's front door. I noticed when Ernie hitched his pants up a little higher on his pot belly, his pistol nearly fell out of his holster. I winced, thinking if it fell it might go off. Tom noticed Ernie's gun and tapped him on the shoulder and pointed to it. Ernie slipped it back in. *Whew!*

The two miners' empty seats were immediately taken by an elderly couple who began complaining about their uncomfortable room. Their main gripe was no television. They also complained about hard pillows. Sound from other rooms. Poor service... even though the bartender came right over and tried to take their order. They disregarded him while still complaining. I tried to tune out their bitching, but they were being too loud making everyone in the bar room uncomfortable. They even made the other three old miners get up and leave. One of their stools got filled by old sheriff Jackson who pulled the whiskey bottle left by the miners over to himself. The bartender handed him a shot glass.

I felt a tap on my shoulder.

"Granny."

"Gwyn, Freesia, and I got a table there in the corner. I think you two need to come sit with us." Granny gave the old couple one of her evil-eye stares and said one word in Romani. The couple went quiet and finally ordered mixed drinks. Now that it was quiet, I was able to tell the bartender we'd be at that table when our food came. I pointed.

"Has something happened?" I asked Granny. "You…"

"Charles, Dear, speak telepathically. There are too many people close by who could hear us."

"Oops. Sorry, Granny. So, what's going on?"

"Dean didn't make it back to his house."

Chapter 29

"What? Is he missing again? But how, Granny? How did you find out?"

"We are sure. Del popped into my room like Tegan came into yours. Gwyn and Freesia were with me. He told us that he went there for a lesson Dean was going to teach him. Del said even Tegan can't feel where Dean is."

Just then the food Bell and I ordered arrived. The bartender brought it over. I said out loud, "Granny, Gwyn, Freesia? You want anything to eat?"

"No, dear. Gwyn and I had some cheese and tea in my room. Freesia?"

"Please. I am hungry again. And sleepy. I am still getting used to not being a cat, but some of my old cat habits are still with me. May I have what they are eating?"

Bell and I had both ordered a BLT sandwich on toasted whole wheat bread. It was tasty.

"Of course, you can." Gwyn told Freesia. "You do need to get used to eating… well, normal food. I will see if I can get the waitress over here."

"Don't bother, Gwyn." I said. "The waitress is through serving. I'll go up to the bar and order it for her. Freesia. Do you want something to drink? Cola? Some other soft drink?"

She just wanted water. I walked up to the bar, got the bartender's attention, and ordered the sandwich for Freesia. Ten minutes later, she was making short work of the sandwich. This time she ate all of it with enjoyment.

When we all finished our late dinner, I went back to the bar to pay for our food and drinks. I also paid for Freesia's. I also wanted to leave a nice tip for the bartender. He'd been working pretty hard for a Christmas Eve, and I knew he would be working harder through the holidays with all the visitors, good and bad.

I had just paid our bill when Ernie came back in. He walked straight up to sheriff Jackson and tapped his back several times. Ernie looked white like he had seen a ghost.

"Sheriff! Sheriff!" Ernie was trying to get the sheriff to put down his glass and turn around. He finally did, with irritation in his eyes.

"Yeah. Okay, Ernie. Stop poking me. What the hell do you want?"

"Sheriff! Sheriff! There… uh, there's a bod… body in ma mine!"

Ernie said that loud enough so everyone remaining in the bar heard him. Including all of us at the table. Except for Freesia who was not paying attention and licking her hands in a cat-like fashion.

Of course, the first thing I thought of was that the body was Dean's. I could also hear several people around us making comments about who they thought it could be. Most figured it was one of the drunk miners who were always hanging around the bar. Since Ernie and Tom were the only two old guys working their mine, it couldn't be Ernie's partner, or he would have said so.

"*Bell. We should get up to that mine before that old sheriff calls in those real sheriffs from Sutter Creek. I hope not, but we need to see if it's Dean in there. Granny, stay here with Gwyn and Freesia and see if Del shows up again with any news.*"

Bell and I headed to our van as quickly as we could without drawing attention. As we drove by Dean's house heading up to the mines, we noticed his front door was open.

"Bell, we better come back here and close his house up for him after we check out the mine. I wouldn't put it past some of those old miners to go in there and grab things they might deem valuable."

Shortly past Dean's house the pavement ended, and it was a twisty dirt road up to the mines. With a few inches of snow on the road, it made for a hard drive. Tom was standing in the open door to their mine, a rifle cradled in his arms. When he saw us drive up, he raised his rifle and pointed it at us. We got out of the van.

I had an idea.

"Hi there. You're Tom, aren't you? Your friend Ernie is with the Sheriff. We're supposed to check things out and report it to the other sheriffs coming from Sutter Creek."

With the rifle still pointed at us, he replied. "Why are ye so important to be here at ma mine?"

Bell smiled at him while telling me telepathically, *"Well, here goes."* She said a few words I'd never heard from her before, and Tom lowered his rifle. "Tom, we are private investigators hired by the Volcano Union Inn to find out about the recent murder at their establishment. They are worried it will affect their business."

"Huh? Really Bell? Private investigators?"

"Well, we are... sort of. Look and learn, my dear lover."

Tom cradled his rifle and motioned for us to go in the mine.

"I don't know what you did, but you need to tell me about it when we get home."

We walked by Tom and entered the mine.

"Bell, we should hurry before the sheriff arrives."

We trotted in up to the mine cart and squeezed by.

Just on the other side of the cart was a body. At least this one wasn't drained of all its bones and blood, especially since there was quite a bit of blood flowing from the crushed head. A woman's body.

"Jeez, Bell. It's not Dean. But..."

"Who is it? It looks like that Wheeler kid's girlfriend. Rhea."

"And who killed her? This is not like the Wheelers' deaths."

"No. And we better get out of here before the sheriff arrives."

As we exited the mine, I said thank you to Tom then recited an Ohlone spell to make him forget we were there. We carefully turned around and drove back down the hill to Dean's house.

"Bell. Look. The door is closed now."

"You think the wind blew it shut? No. It couldn't be. There's no wind."

We got out of the van.

"Uh… look over there."

In front of the old vacant house next door to Dean's place was that new white Mercedes, the car the Wheeler's son had been driving with his girlfriend, Rhea.

"Charles. Someone was looking out the window a second ago. We better protect ourselves."

Bell and I recited protective spells, like a forcefield, around ourselves then stepped onto the porch. Before opening the door, we stood there quietly trying to hear any noise inside. Quiet.

Like a police swat team, I quickly opened the door and ran inside ready to use whatever warlock means I could muster in short notice.

Empty.

No one was there.

"I was sure I saw someone look out the window at us," Bell said.

"I don't doubt that. Someone was here and might have been going through Dean's belongings. Whoever it was, must have some kind of power, like a wizard, and disappeared."

"I wish I got a better look at whoever it was. I do think it was a woman, though. It didn't look like Tegan, though. Too short."

Just then we heard the roar of the Mercedes outside. We ran to the window and saw the car spin around in the snow and accelerate downhill, nearly running into Sheriff Jackson's Jeep Cherokee. We watched and heard as the sheriff and his passenger, Ernie, went by swearing a blue streak. Probably because they were almost run into by the escaping girl.

"Bell. Did you see that? That's the same girl we saw in the mine. That's Rhea! What the hell's going on?"

Chapter 30

"So, Bell, let's go back in and see if we can find out what that Rhea, or whoever she is, was looking for."

We went back in. Looking around we saw that Dean had done quite a bit to get his fire damage cleaned up. So far, he had used his wizard power the straighten up his front room and kitchen. I glanced into his bedroom and noticed it was only half done.

"Bell. Dean never finished his cleaning. He... oh crud! Look." I pointed to the floor by his charred closet door.

"Oh my. Dean's wand. Another one broken. If he's trapped somewhere without a wand, he might not be able to get back."

"Let's hope he has another."

"He seemed to keep extras in that suitcase under his bed." I got down on all fours and looked. "Gone. His suitcase is gone."

"Maybe he took it with him. I don't think the girl took it. You know, maybe that was what she was looking for."

I reached down to pick up the two pieces of Dean's wand.

"Ouch!" I dropped them. "Those pieces really gave me a shock!"

"There must be power still in them. Are you okay?"

"Yeah, but I got a quick vision of something. Now that I know what that feels like, I'm going to try to hold them again."

This time I grabbed both together and held them tightly in my hand. I started shaking. Bell grabbed my free hand, and she felt the shock and started shaking. Both of our rings flashed brightly.

And we disappeared.

And reappeared.

"Jeez, Bell. What just happened?" I leaned back against a large sugar pine tree.

Bell was quiet and collapsed on the pine needle covered ground in a sitting position.

"Bell! Bell! Are you okay?"

"Yeah. Yeah. That was just too strange, even for us. I feel weak."

"I do too. Uh… this place looks awfully familiar."

"It is. Look around. We're in the same valley. Volcano."

"Are we in Dean's wizard world?"

"I don't think so. This looks different. We must be in a different time."

"Weird. Same place, but no buildings. Now. How do we get back?"

"The easiest way is through the Masonic cave portal."

"Dean!" We both exclaimed. As usual, he appeared out of

nowhere and scared us.

"Here, I brought you water. You need to drink." Dean handed us a soft deer skin container with a wooden stopper. He pulled it out and handed it to us.

"Where did you get this?" Bell asked as she took a big drink then handed it to me.

"From the Miwok Indians who live here. There are a few springs around here with very cold refreshing water that is sacred to them. There are also a lot of game here that the Indians hunt, and many thousands of acorns the women grind for their delicious flat bread. Unfortunately, in less than a hundred years from this time, the springs will be overused during the gold rush and get sealed with mine tailings. They will all dry up. When the miners come, the Indians will leave and go to higher ground away from the dirt and noise."

"What are you doing here? And how did we get here?" Bell and I had so many questions to ask.

"Ah. I left that broken wand hoping you would pick it up. I put some magic on it to bring you here. Your rings helped. I hope it was not painful. I know how my wands and transferences can make you uncomfortable."

"It did," I said, nodding my head. "But with our rings glowing so much, we had to perservere."

Bell asked, "Del and Tegan couldn't locate you. What happened to you?"

"Ah. I was attacked on my way home and made a quick disappearance to get away. I didn't want to have my attacker follow me to the wizard world where my family is, so I went only part way back in time to hide. And maybe catch my attacker if she somehow followed me."

"She?" Bell and I said at the same time.

"You have met her. She was that very upset young woman who was the Wheeler boy's girlfriend."

"That mousey little girl?" Bell asked. "We just saw her dead and bleeding in Ernie and Tom's mine. Then we saw her again driving away in that white Mercedes."

"Yes. She put up quite a front. Fooled all of us. Even used a doppelgänger to make everyone think she was dead. No, my... uh, Rhea is not dead. At least I hope not." Dean said that last sentence so quietly we didn't hear it.

"Holy... uh... was she hired by the Wheelers? Did they know who she is? What she could do?" I asked.

"No. They had no idea who she was. They just thought she was... like you said, Bell, a mousey little girl who was their son's girlfriend. She is from the wizard world. She is working alone."

"How did she escape the plague?" Bell asked.

"She was probably only eight or nine and in your world attending school when the plague happened. It was easy for her to follow Del into the post plague wizard world. She had been there recently before."

"I thought you said the plague was several hundred years ago," I questioned.

"It was. But that was wizard time. Really. I have not lived two or three hundred years. In your time, and in reality, I am only eighty-five years old. Actually," Dean chuckled unsmiling. "I am younger than your grandmother, Yana." Dean got serious again. "Now. Let us go rest in the Indian village. Most of them are back in the Sacramento Valley this time of year, but a few of them stay here. Charles, you will find it interesting."

"Really? How?"

"You will see. You will see."

After drinking some more from the deer skin canteen, Bell and I felt much better. We followed Dean for a quarter mile or so along a narrow trail that ended in a clearing with a dozen bark teepees. Only one or two of the smaller looked lived in and all but one of the larger ones were empty. The largest teepee had a bear skin door hanging down and partially folded up. Smoke was coming out of the top of the teepee.

"Charles, Bell, come in to warm up and meet the shaman."

We all stooped to enter the teepee. Layers of thick roughhewn bark made for a solid looking and watertight building. A small warming fire, lined with stones was centered on the floor. On the floor by the walls were several dark bear skins. Sitting cross legged on one was a very old looking Indian. He looked up at me with his small eyes and smiled, making his leathery face fill with wrinkles. I could see from the twinkle in his eyes that he was alert and intelligent. He also knew right away that we would not understand each other's languages. He began signing.

I understood. It was like when grandfather couldn't talk to me because of my weak medicine bag and signed. Speaking of which, the shaman had a medicine bag almost identical to mine.

He signed. *"Welcome. Sit. Warm yourselves."*

I translated. He motioned we sit across from him. We sat down on a large black furry bear skin. *"Ah. Not bad. Very comfortable,"* I said to Bell telepathically. The shaman smiled again and nodded at us.

I signed. "*Thank you. So honored to meet you. My name.* Charles." I said my name out loud. "*This my woman. My friend.* Bell." I said her name out loud too.

He smiled at Bell and signed. "*Beautiful.*" Then he was quiet for several seconds, looking off into space as if he was remembering someone in his past. He looked back to me. "*My name.* Molimo." He said his name out loud. Then he signed, "*He who walks in shadows.*" I nodded to let him know I understood.

Molimo then held his medicine bag and motioned for me to sit next to him. I moved over and sat by him.

He signed for me to close my eyes and hold on to my medicine bag. I did and felt his hand on my forehead.

In what must have been less than a second to me, I felt I was able to communicate with Molimo in his own language. Telepathically. I also saw… or maybe I dreamed of Grandfather and something about a bright light. A familiar bright light.

When I opened my eyes, I was sitting alone. Molimo was gone. Bell and Dean were gone.

I got up and went outside. It was dark and Molimo, Bell, and Dean were sitting on logs next to a large fire pit eating something an older Indian woman must have cooked. I sat down next to Bell. The woman handed me a wood bowl with some kind of steaming stew in it along with an acorn flour flat bread that looked like a small, thick tortilla.

"Bell. Was I out for a while?"

"You were out for five hours."

"You're kidding. I felt like I only closed my eyes for a second."

"*Ah. Young shaman. Charles. You must eat and drink. Build up your strength. Your time journey is about to be over. But another will come soon for you and your woman, Bell."* Molimo spoke to me in his own language telepathically, and I understood him. *"You will rest in my home tonight, then follow Dean back to your time early before the sun rises. An evil spirit will arrive soon after you leave looking for you three. I am ready for her."*

"Molimo. You know about our time?" I was curious.

"I have traveled there myself. Not with my body. With my mind." He tapped his head then picked up his pipe and tapped that. I thought I had smelled marijuana when we first met him. *"You want to know how I know your future. Yes? I cannot describe it. You will know how one day. Now. Eat. Drink more water. Then rest."*

The stew, chunks of deer meat and some kind of root vegetable, thickened with acorn flour, was actually good. The flat bread was as good as Dean said it was. Bell, Dean, and I finished eating and we drank a lot of water. I was worried I would have to get up in the middle of the night to take a leak in the forest.

The three of us went into Molimo's teepee and curled up on the bear skins and immediately went to sleep.

Dean roused us four hours later. It was still dark. We followed him down the path to the Masonic cave.

"We must be careful… and quiet. There is no path to the upper cave like there is in your time. We will have to climb a little. Also, in this time in history, bears have been known to hibernate in some of the caves. We do not want to disturb them."

I could smell the ripe odor of bear scat and urine as we passed one cave on the way uphill, and we all kept quiet. After a short climb, we entered the Masonic cave. Dean pulled out another wand from his pocket and pointed it at the back wall. The portal opened and we started to enter.

We were just passing through the portal when our path got blocked.

It was Rhea, the young sorceress.

Chapter 31

She stood there with her arms crossed. I was expecting her to attack and already had my hand on my medicine bag. She didn't.

Dean put his wand back in his pocket and walked up to her. He had his arms crossed too. He was between Rhea and me and Bell, which would make it hard for Bell and me to use any witch/warlock or shaman powers on the sorceress. I was watching her face to see if I could tell what her intentions were. I was surprised when she smiled at Dean. Dean smiled back.

And then they hugged.

"Wha… Who… Uh… Dean?" I stammered.

"Oh. Sorry, my friends. Let me introduce Rhea. Garrett's half-sister from England. Rhea, I know you already know Bell and Charles. Ha." Dean laughed. "I can see you both are confused and have many questions."

"You ain't just whistling Dixie," I said.

"I beg your pardon?" Dean questioned.

"Sorry. My dad used to say that. So, what's going on?"

"Rhea is not a sorceress. She is, like Garrett mentioned, a wizardess. I have known about her for a long, long time. Much longer than Garrett."

"But she looks so young," Bell said.

Rhea answered. "I am not that young. I am younger than my half-brother, Garrett, but… well, look."

As we watched, Rhea changed from a young blond eighteen-year-old, to a much older gray-haired woman of at least seventy… maybe eighty. "See. This is the real me."

I was at a loss for words. I just stared with my mouth open.

Bell, however, spoke right up. "Why the deception?"

"I am so sorry I could not confide in you," Dean replied. "Rhea has been working undercover. We have known for a long time about the assassins and have been working for decades to find out their source. We felt we were close to them with those scam artist Wheelers, who thought the two with them were real followers of theirs. They somehow brought along money… a whole lot of money… and they gave it to the Wheelers to get in their good graces and have a place to hang out. That is how they were able to purchase all the cars. It was that couple, spellbound like the Reverend was, who convinced the Wheelers to go to Volcano to find Del and Dria. I got caught up in it and got on their list. I am sure you both are too. Somehow, they knew that Del and Dria drove here to be with me. How? Maybe through the power in my wand."

"And here I thought Rhea was the source. The possessor, like you said a while ago," I said. Then asked, "Rhea. Who is that dead girl in the mine who looks like you... uh, when you appeared young?"

"That was an illusion, but I did not do that. That was not me but someone who could shape shift to look like me. Whoever it is thought I really was a young woman and used that image of me to fake a murder. I've actually been here waiting for Dean for nearly an hour. No one died in that mine. Those drunken miners now probably believe they were seeing things."

"That's a relief," Bell said. "It sure fooled us."

I was thinking, then said, "Couldn't the possessor know you were a wizardess? Weren't you carrying and using a wand?"

"No. I gave my wand to Dean to hide. If I had it on me, I would have been found out long ago. Willing myself to be appear as a mousy and not-too-intelligent young blond to everyone worked out quite well. It was very easy to ingratiate myself to Nicolas Wheeler and travel with them all. I am very sorry Nicolas had to die like his parents. He was ill and would have passed away in a year or so, but he would have had a better life without them... at least for a while." Rhea let out a big sigh and I was sure I saw a tear drop from her eyes. "Oh. And it was not Tegan who killed Nicolas."

"So, Dean, Rhea, what do we do now?" Bell asked. "We're here in your world. Should we get Tegan, Del and his children, and all try to draw the possessor into a trap?"

"Not Tegan," Dean said. "It is too bright for her."

I remembered seeing Dean's image on Gwyn's boat. "Dean, you showed your projected image to Granny and Gwen and moved her boat to the Stockton harbor. I remember you mentioning that Tegan could do the same. Can't she help that way?"

"You are right. She has moved around, although invisibly, as she told me, to watch over Del, Marty, and Dria. I will contact her then we can go gather up the others. Using their new wands along with mine we should be able to send a strong signal that may bring the possessor to us. As I have said before, fingers crossed."

While Dean attempted to contact Tegan, Bell and I walked over to one of the small springs and slaked our time-travel thirst. A trickle of cold water came out of a tiny fissure in the limestone that had minerals of some kind around and down from the opening. The spring water had a slight mineral taste.

"Bell. This water really tastes good. Too bad the miners in the 1800s destroyed the springs around here. Look down there. That's why the area got mined so heavily."

"Flakes of gold. Quite a few. The spring's source must run through a vein of gold."

"Too bad there wasn't a way for us to keep this from being destroyed."

Bell hit my arm. "Charles! Don't even think it. We cannot change history."

"Ouch. Sorry."

"There's Dean. He looks worried. Dean. What's wrong?"

"I cannot locate Tegan here. She may have traveled to another time outside of my mental reach. Del, Rhea, and I plan to search through time for her. Can I count on you two to stay here with Marty and Dria? I do not want my whole family traveling through time and space all at once. Too risky."

Bell agreed. I agreed too, but I had a question. "If you three use your wands to look for Tegan, won't the possessor sense the signals and come here… or follow you?"

"You are right. However, I did advise Marty and Dria to light their wands to alert me and the others if the possessor makes an appearance. We could be here in a split second. You two should also be prepared… just in case."

"We will," I said. "Along with my grandfather's help."

Del and Rhea walked over and stood on each side of Dean, wands at the ready. They disappeared.

Bell and I walked over to where Marty and Dria were sitting on a fallen tree. They had their heads in their hands and looked dejected. We sat down beside them.

"So, guys," I said. "What's wrong? You want to go with the others. Don't you?"

"I could help so much finding grandmother." Dria, acting like the eighteen old girl she is, was pouting.

"I understand we shouldn't all go, but I wish we could." Marty, the older of the two, wasn't pouting, but did look depressed.

"You two do know what you're supposed to do if someone we don't know shows up? Don't you?"

"Yeah. Yeah. Uncle Dean told us to signal him if something happens," Dria, still pouting, said. "So here we have to sit and wait… and wait."

"Dear children. You do not have to wait anymore. I am here."

"Grandmother?" Marty and Dria yelled. Like Dean, Tegan appeared out of nowhere.

"Tegan?" Bell and I questioned. I narrowed my eyes and stared at her. She was walking toward Marty and Dria, who stood up and were ready to give her a hug.

I spoke to Bell telepathically. *"Something is wrong! That Tegan is holding her wand in her left hand and upside down. I remember Tegan being right-handed."*

"You're right! Quick. We must stop her from touching those two!"

"Marty! Dria! Stop!" I yelled and Bell and I jumped between Tegan and the kids.

Bell whispered in Marty's ear. He raised his wand and it lit, then he dropped it as it became hot and turned to ash on the ground.

Chapter 32

Tegan changed. It was not Tegan, Del's mother, anymore. Her appearance went from the good-looking pale sort of goth looking middle-aged woman we were used to seeing to a wrinkled old-looking hag with a fiery red eye. Her leathery skin looked like it had been severely burned and healed over years ago. Her gray hair looked like it had never been washed and hung in thin strands around a bald spot on the top of her head. She wore a threadbare kaftan that was so dirty you couldn't make out a pattern. She was barefoot.

"Well, well, well. What have we here?" she asked, talking out of the right side of her mouth. Her left side seemed stuck in place as if she had a stroke. She answered her own question. "Oh. Young wizards. Oh. You'll be so easy to take care of. Now…"

Dean, Del, and Rhea appeared next to us.

"Oh. Now. I finally got you all together... at last! At last!"

Del spoke up in anger. "Who are you? And what have you done with my mother?"

"Oh. Yes. Your mother. I have her bound in another time and place where the morning sun will do to her what she did to me. Hee hee." Her cackle was disconcerting. "Of course, she probably won't live out the day once the light starts cooking her. Oh. I'm so sorry you will lose your mother so soon after getting back together with her. Oh. By the way, your uncle knows who I am. Right... Dean?"

"Meg! You... you crazy ugly bitch. I was told you were dead!" Dean pulled his wand out. But before he could use it, Meg's left eye immediately turned white, and a narrow beam shot out of it hitting Dean's wand and burning it like she had done to Marty's. Dean yelped and dropped the hot branch. It turned to ash on the ground. Meg's eye became red again. Del, Rhea, and Dria had their wands out too, but quickly put them away before Meg noticed.

"Oh. So sorry Dean Prentiss. Did I burn your hand?" With only half of Meg's face and mouth working, her act of a pouting apology made her look more grotesque than she already was. "Now. Who are these two? More wizards? No? Ah. Yes. A pretty boy warlock and a lovely witch! Too bad you blundered along with these soon to be ex-wizards. Now I'll have to use both of you to do my bidding. Your kind are so easy to control... as you've found out with my other assassins."

Dean's anger was rising. I worried he would try to do something to Meg without thinking. I kept my hand on my medicine bag and kept whispering soothing words to calm

Dean's mind. He relaxed.

Knowing that wizards and even the sorceress are not able to speak or hear telepathically, while Meg was talking, or rather taunting Dean, Bell and I were conversing in our minds, planning what to do. We knew we could not be controlled by her, but we decided to fake it. Try to catch Meg off guard. But first…

"So, Meg. Before you… uh, enslave us, how did you survive that plague you started? We heard that you died along with all the wizards in this world. Obviously, you didn't. Or did you?"

"Oh. Yes. Tegan spread that rumor. She didn't stick around to make sure I was dead. So, I feigned my death. Oh. So easy to do for my… for our kind. I willed myself into suspended animation. Unfortunately, while in that state, the… this damn wizard, here, came back and started a fire to purify the land! I did not wake in time! My appearance is Dean's fault! Oh! Dean. Who will no longer be with us very soon! I will get my sweet revenge! Finally! Now, my dear assassins! It is time to act!"

Act. Yes. Act we must.

Because only half of Meg's face worked, her one good eye turned white as she looked at me and Bell. I felt a slight tingling sensation that I first thought must be from Meg's attempt at controlling us. But it was coming from our rings. So, with my hand on my medicine bag, and my other hand holding Bell's, we pretended to be in her control. Dean and the others looked on in horror.

"Oh! Now! My lovely minions! Use your new abilities and kill them all!"

Bell and I slowly walked toward the wizards. I winked at Dean. He caught on, but now acted like his time was up.

Before we could turn and attack Meg, two things happened that caused her to pause and get distracted.

First. Grandfather. Peter Red Feather appeared next to me in his ghostly form. Not just to me, but to everyone. Second. Tegan's image appeared in front of Dean, Del, and his kids. It was also a ghostly image, like the one I saw of Dean on Gwyn's boat. Everyone saw her too.

Meg seemed shocked to see both the ghostly images, but immediately tried to use her white-hot stare with her one good eye aiming it at first Tegan, then Grandfather. Her burning vision went right through both images, igniting a pair of trees behind them.

I felt Grandfather's hand on my shoulder. His other hand on Bell's shoulder. Tegan appeared to put her arms around each of her relations. Then she and Grandfather glided toward Meg hovering just above the ground. Bell and I then turned to face her. Meg's half mouth opened and stuttered. "Wha… who… oh, shit! You can't be here! And you two are not under my control?"

Del, Rhea, and Dria pulled out their wands. Dean really didn't need one. He just lifted his hand.

Bell raised her hand and just said "No, Meg." I kept hold of my medicine bag.

Meg's one eye again turned from red to white. She was ready to strike.

But couldn't. Grandfather's spirit stood directly in front of her. Tegan's ghostly image was behind her. Dean's raised hand shot out a lightning bolt, as did the other's wands.

Bell's raised hand also shot out a bolt. I was astounded she could do that but followed suit. I raised my free hand and was able to do it too. I had no idea we could do that. It had to be Tegan. Or Grandfather. Or both of them.

Attacking Meg in concert made her collapse, falling back into the ghostly arms of Tegan. Dead. This time really dead.

Tegan's magic gently laid her down and we watched as Meg drifted down and disappeared into the earth.

Tegan's image came over to Dean. She couldn't speak but she motioned for all of us to follow her.

The sun was about to rise soon, and the dark sky had already started to lighten up. We started to follow Tegan, but her image disappeared. Dean looked worried. "We have to find Tegan before the sun comes up. I don't want to lose her… again. Everyone. We have to spread out and find…"

"Who do you need to find, my dear brother?"

"Tegan!"

This was not her image. It was the real Tegan. Like Dean showing up out of nowhere in Volcano, Tegan did the same, then walked up and hugged Dean.

"Tegan. How did you get loose? Meg said you were bound so the sun would burn you up. Tegan! The sun is rising. Get into the cavern. Quickly."

"Dear brother. That is no longer necessary. With Meg's death, my bonds were broken and my aversion to the sun is over. I can be with you all any time day or night."

Grandfather's spirit was still standing by me with his hands on our shoulders. "Tegan, I would like you to meet my grandfather. This is Peter Red Feather. He is my guiding shaman spirit. Grandfather, please meet Tegan Rhees."

He bowed to Tegan.

Tegan curtsied. "I am honored to meet you, Mister Red Feather."

Grandfather turned to me. "My dear grandson. I must now return to the earth. I will see you again if and when the need arises." He took his hands off me and Bell, raised his right hand to signal goodbye to the others... and disappeared.

Dean came over to me and Bell and let out a big sigh. "I think it is time for us all to return to our time. Rhea. You want to join us?"

"I would love to, but I must be away to my side of the world. Back to Dunwich. Goodbye everyone. I hope to see you all again someday." She raised her wand and disappeared.

"Dean. Is the portal this way?" I pointed toward a hillside.

"It is, but we don't need it now."

"What? How?"

"Look at your rings."

Glowing. Glowing brightly.

"Follow us."

Dean and Tegan held hands and disappeared. Del, Marty, and Dria did the same.

Bell and I felt the electrical charge, took deep breaths, and...

Epilogue

We arrived back in the town of Volcano, in our own time, appearing inside Dean's house where we joined Tegan, Del, and his kids in the living room to warm ourselves in front of the fire. Dean went into the kitchen to make a large batch of hot chocolate.

Bell and I were feeling anxious to leave, but we were very thirsty from the time travel. We asked for some water.

"Hold off for a few more minutes. This hot chocolate, with a dash of cinnamon will do you much better than several glasses of water. It is also good and will warm you up on this cold day."

And a few minutes later Dean came into the living area and handed mugs of chocolate all around. He was right. A few sips and Bell and I felt much better and could relax. We could all relax.

Bell and I sat there and finished our chocolate while the others were talking and going over where every one of them were going now that the current assassin problem was over. We felt like we needed to leave them alone to continue catching up on their family history.

"Dean. We really need to get back to the hotel. We want to let Granny and Gwyn and Freesia know we are back and okay. Everyone. We will probably be leaving today to head back to Santa Cruz."

"Charles, Bell," Del said. "Thank you so much for helping. Marty, Dria, and I will see you there. We also want to get home to Santa Cruz and clean up my house. I know those Wheelers really messed it up. Drive carefully. It is still icy out there."

We shook hands all around. Tegan came over and gave us hugs. Bell and I walked out into the cold and down the hill back to the hotel.

It was early Christmas morning and breakfast was in full swing. Granny, Gwyn, and Freesia were sitting at a round table in the middle of the restaurant. There were two empty chairs.

Granny got up and gave us both big hugs. "I'm so glad you're back… and safe. Gwyn…"

"I sensed something had happened to you," Gwyn cut in. "I knew you were far away. A time far away. When the sun came up, all seemed well, and I could breathe easier. I told Yana all was taken care of, and you would be back soon. So, we saved you two chairs."

"We'll tell you all about what happened… after we eat. We're starved after our journeys."

"Go. They are still serving that good ham, as Freesia can attest." Freesia had a mouthful of ham and just smiled and nodded.

After cleaning our plates, we started planning our day.

I suggested, "I would love to leave this morning. Gwyn, can I drive you three to your boat in Stockton?"

"That would be lovely."

"You'll probably be home long before we get back to the harbor," Granny said. "We'll probably get in too late, so I'll spend the night with Gwyn and Freesia. I'll contact you tomorrow to pick me up."

Bell and I put everyone's bags in the van. We all checked out and left an hour after breakfast. After dropping Granny, Gwyn, and Freesia by the Stockton dock where Gwyn's boat was moored, Bell and I headed home. Four hours later we were back in Santa Cruz. We first stopped at Day's Market in Seabright to pick up a baguette, brie and some cheddar, and a bottle of Pelican Ranch Cab, then went home and collapsed on the sofa with our wine, bread, and cheese. We could unpack later… if we didn't fall asleep first. After our second glass of wine, we leaned back on the sofa and dozed.

When we woke, the sun was setting.

"Bell. Let's get our bags out of the van and unpack. Here's hoping we can relax for a while now."

"And when Yana comes back, we could go out for a belated Christmas dinner at the Crow's Nest."

"Excellent idea."

We went out to the van, and I grabbed my backpack and Bell picked up her suitcase. We brought them in the house and dropped them on the bed.

Bell immediately opened her suitcase and emptied it. She started throwing most of her clothes into the hamper in my closet.

I started to do the same.

But...

"Uh... Bell. What's this?" I held up an eight-inch-long stick with a forked end.

"That looks like one of Dean's wands."

As I held it, the end started to glow.

Our rings started to glow too.

We felt a pull. I dropped the wand.

As quickly as it started, it stopped. I threw the wand back into my backpack and tossed it into the back of my closet.

"No!" We both exclaimed. "No more! We need some rest!"

Author's Notes

Many years ago, I did visit the gold rush mining town of Volcano. I fell in love with the quaint village, the historical buildings, and the countryside around that one block of the main street. I even thought about buying an old home there to be part of the town's history.

Mining started in that area simply by panning for gold in the creeks and streams. The highly destructive placer (hydrolic) mining took over in the 1850s and was used for decades. Forests, streams, and hillsides were reduced to rock and rubble. Drag-line dredging of the creeks existed into the 1930s, causing more damage to the environment. Only one or two hard rock mines and diggings exist in the area. The damage in Volcano is now hidden by trees and with an amphitheater where plays are performed during the summer months.

The streets, the St. George hotel and the Volcano Union Pub and Inn, and the small businesses are real. The homes I describe are fictitious. Any hard rock mines in the area are far from the locations I described. None are up Emigrant Road past "Dean's" house.

The two graveyards, the Pioneer Cemetery and the Catholic Cemetery are where I described in the story. These do date back to the gold rush days.

Volcano did have thousands of miners and families living there at one point. As the gold ran out and was harder to mine, the place nearly became a ghost town. There are only a little over a hundred permanent residents there now.

There are four major cave systems and caverns hidden in the limestone along the hills of the gold rush country. Two of them are privately run, one is a state park, and Black Chasm, by Volcano, is a National Natural Landmark. It is large and quite spectacular with its unusual formations.

The Masonic Cave, on the other hand is very plain. The parking area is set up as a park with tables for picnicking. And, yes, there is a sign that says to beware of rattlesnakes. The cave is closer to Volcano than Black Chasm and is a local landmark. There are several caves that honeycomb the limestone hillside, and the topmost is where the Masonic meetings were held. And, as my story mentions, only five meetings occurred there in the 1850s. The Masons soon moved into a new hall in town, sharing it with the Odd Fellows. It was sure to be much warmer and dryer than the cold, damp cave they started in.

In Santa Cruz, my hometown, the information about the earthquake and how many of Santa Cruz's businesses survived during the aftermath is all true. I lived it.

The Catalyst is a real concert hall and restaurant and is still in the same location. However, my story about the benefit concert was fictional, as were the bands (except the punk band was similar to one I played in from 1979 to 1982 in the same venue).

Charles Blue and Bell will be back in

Time On Our Hands.
Coming 2024

www.ingramcontent.com/pod-product-compliance
Lightning Source LLC
LaVergne TN
LVHW041702070526
838199LV00045B/1161